a30118   D0231294

SCENES FROM BOURGEOIS LIFE

'I admire Mervyn Jones for his scrupulous observation of people: nobody can more unerringly set a human scene, choose the right flat words, measure a pause, evaluate a silence or a glance' – *Guardian*

The stories in this first collection by one of Britain's favourite novelists examine situations which are not unique and which, sadly, may not even appear unusual. But each is the tip of an iceberg of frustration, unhappiness and confusion; each, in the hands of a writer of Mervyn Jones's calibre, provides a powerful drama of the aridity which can afflict those living the supposedly good life of the bourgeoisie.

These are stories about infidelity, greed, politics, boredom, incest. But through all of these very different situations run common themes of the personal and social unhappiness which erupts when middle-class lives based on habit and unthinking assumption reach crisis point. The shallowness of material success, the lack of rapport between husbands and wives, the oppressiveness of conventional morality – these are themes which have distinguished the author's novels. In short-story format they are treated with deftness and conciseness to produce an acid but sympathetic statement about people's relationships with each other.

SCENES FROM BOURGEOIS LIFE

MERVYN JONES

QUARTET BOOKS   LONDON

476016049

01560102

First published by Quartet Books Limited 1976
27 Goodge Street, London W1P 1FD

Copyright © 1976 by Mervyn Jones

ISBN 0 704 32115 7

Typesetting by Bedford Typesetters Ltd

Printed in Great Britain by litho by The Anchor Press Ltd
and bound by Wm Brendon & Son Ltd
both of Tiptree, Essex

SCENES FROM BOURGEOIS LIFE

THE SYNDROME

At ten o'clock in the morning, when Constance Garrard had just come in from taking the dog for his walk on Hampstead Heath, the telephone rang. She answered briskly, giving her number. She was expecting the plumber to let her know whether he would be able to replace a defective valve today. Expecting . . . well, he had promised to ring yesterday, but a day more or less made no difference to plumbers.

'Hello . . . Connie?'

It wasn't the plumber; it was Julia Bradley. 'Oh, Julia. How are you?'

'Fine. Well, all right. How are you?'

'Fine.'

'Connie, I'm sorry to ring up like this, but do you think I could come round and see you?'

'Of course,' Constance said. 'Now?'

'Well, if it's inconvenient . . .'

'No, no. You just pop round. I'll make coffee.'

It was certain, Constance thought as she cleared away the breakfast plates and cups, that the plumber would arrive just when they sat down to coffee. It was also certain that Julia had a domestic problem of her own. Julia was notoriously helpless with things like plumbing and electricity, didn't even remember the names of local repair firms, and had relied on Constance ever since they had both lived in London, which was more than twenty years. Evidently, it would be one of those days. As well as the plumber, and helping Julia, the dog had a touch of eczema and the car had a slow leak in a front tyre. Besides, Alan had gone to Cardiff for the day. Although Constance normally didn't see her husband all day and quite often all evening too, she had a vague sense of isolation when he was away from London and out of touch.

Julia arrived, not surprisingly since she lived nearby, within ten minutes. She was neatly turned out, as usual, in a black dress. In her sweater and trousers, Constance felt slightly at a disadvantage. When they had been girls – they were cousins – Julia had always been better dressed, as well as undeniably more attractive. Constance also thought, however, that the predictable black dresses were rather unimaginative. Julia, being a classical English blonde, had grasped at an early age that she looked well in black, and had stuck to it, both for day and evening wear. Now that she was . . . they were . . . no longer young, a re-think was overdue.

'I'm sorry about this,' Julia said. Like most people who seek help, she was profuse with her apologies.

'Not a bit,' Constance said cheerfully. 'It's nice to see you. Alan's had to dash off to Wales, so I'm alone all day, till about midnight I should think.'

'I see.'

The dog, who knew Julia well, jumped up to be petted.

'Hello, Prince,' Julia said dutifully. 'How's old Prince?'

'He's starting his bloody eczema again,' Constance said. 'They're worse than kids, honestly. But there you are, Alan's got to have a dog.'

They had coffee in the kitchen, a big room with double doors to the garden.

'Well,' Constance asked, hoping to get it over with, 'what's the trouble?'

Julia didn't answer at once. Her large blue eyes roved round the room, in a fugitive manner which was peculiarly her own.

'It really is trouble, you know,' she said at last.

'Come on, out with it.'

'Denis is leaving me.'

Constance stared. Her first reaction, she told Alan later, was of

complete incredulity: literal incredulity, as though she'd been told
that Denis was turning into a monkey.

'He can't be,' she said.

'He is, I'm afraid.'

'You mean you've had a row?'

'No, no row. Just . . . an announcement.'

'When was this?'

'Last night. I phoned you, but there was no reply.'

'We went to the theatre. But look here, what did he say?'

'He's leaving me,' Julia repeated, like a child entrusted with a
message.

'And what did you say?'

'Not very much. I didn't know what to say.'

'Well, what's the position now? Has he gone to work today, or
what?'

'No, you see . . . I shouldn't have said he's leaving me, exactly. He
has left me. Last night.'

'What, just walked out?'

'Well, he took a suitcase. And he didn't walk, he phoned for a
minicab. But he went, yes.'

'This is fantastic,' Constance said.

'Well, you see, he's got somebody else.'

'He has, has he? You'd better tell me about that.'

'I can't tell you very much. I had no idea, you see, until he told me
last night. She's called Terry. She works in advertising.'

'OK, he's having an affair. It's very nasty, but it does happen.
You'll have to decide how to handle it.'

'Oh no, it isn't just an affair. He's in love with this Terry.'

'He says.'

'It sounded like it, the way he said it. And it's been going on for
over a year.'

'Over a year! And you mean you had no idea?'

'Well, Connie, how does one? It's only in books you find letters
in his pocket and that kind of thing. It never crossed my mind. I
mean, he's often out in the evening, he always has been. So he's been
seeing her . . . I realise that now. And trying to decide what to do.
Feeling awful.'

'He says.'

'No, why shouldn't he feel awful? We've been married all this time.'

3

'Oh yes . . . I didn't mean . . .' Constance felt, oddly, that Julia had an advantage over her. She had been reflecting on this unprecedented situation for twelve hours, or whatever it was – whereas she, Constance, was still trying to grasp it.

She asked: 'What else did he say about her – Terry?'

'Not much. Oh, I asked him how old she is. She's twenty-four.'

The phone rang. It was the plumber; he would come round right away, if it suited.

'I'd better go,' Julia said, finishing her coffee.

'You needn't. It's just the plumber.'

'No, I mean, there isn't any more to say, is there? I just had to tell somebody. Thank you, Connie.'

'I haven't been much use, I'm afraid. I feel . . . it's all so incredible.' Julia smiled sadly. 'Yes, it is, isn't it?'

'Now look, do ring me again if there's any developments. Or pop round, any time.'

'I'm not expecting any developments. It's happened, hasn't it?'

'Don't be so despondent, Julia. I don't see that anything conclusive has happened, certainly not. Anyway, we must have a real talk about it. When Alan gets back.'

After Julia had gone Constance dealt with the plumber, put ointment on the dog's ear, and changed the tyre. Then she tried to think about what could be done for Julia, but nothing occurred to her and she decided to rely on talking to Alan. In the afternoon, feeling restless, she took the tube to Oxford Street and did some shopping. Though she didn't normally spend much on clothes and seldom bought on impulse, she committed herself to a striking and expensive long dress. It struck her that she ought to have made Julia come shopping and persuaded her to buy a dress like this. The thought of Julia musing through the day was distressing. When she got home, Constance phoned and asked her to come over for a scratch supper. But Julia said she had a headache; she hadn't slept much last night, so she would go to bed early.

Constance had the scratch supper herself, tried to read, couldn't settle to it, and watched television. At about ten o'clock she had a sudden desire to see what the new dress looked like. She went upstairs and put it on. She did look good in it, she decided. She hadn't been proud of her appearance as a young woman, but she liked to think that she'd become . . . not exactly more attractive . . . more

4

distinctive in middle age. Turning regretfully away from the mirror, she paused for a minute on the stairs, assuming a welcoming pose. It would be nice if Alan came in now, she thought. But he didn't, then or later. Eventually, when she had to reconcile herself to the fact that the last train from Cardiff must have arrived, Constance went to bed.

She was awakened, while it was still dark, by the sound of Alan coming into the bedroom.

'Is that you, darling?'

'No, it's your husband,' he said.

'Ha-ha, funny joke.'

He leaned over the bed and kissed her. When he was about to draw away, she clasped her arms round his neck and prolonged the kiss.

'Well, well, well,' he said. 'Missed me?'

'Yes, I missed you.'

'I got involved in a dinner, so I took the night sleeper.'

'You could have phoned.'

'I didn't think you'd worry.'

'I didn't worry. I missed you. What time is it?'

'Half past six. I think I'll have a bath.'

'I'll make some breakfast.'

'No, no, darling, you go back to sleep.'

'I can't, now. Anyway, you've woken Prince up, he'll have to be let out.'

At this hour, everything seemed very quiet. Constance wondered whether Julia was awake; probably she was. It must be hard to get used to waking alone. Standing in the garden with the dog, watching for the first grey light of a winter day, Constance shivered. She turned on all the lights on the ground floor, and also the radio.

Alan appeared in his bath-robe.

'How was the trip, then?' she asked.

'Oh, fine. All very friendly. There's a really good Italian restaurant in Cardiff, you'd be surprised.'

'Good.'

'What've you been doing?'

'Nothing much.' She wanted to tell Alan about the new dress, but the moment didn't seem right.

'Did you remember about Prince's ointment?'

'Yes, I did that.'

He looked up quickly from his cornflakes.

'What's wrong, Connie? You're not actually cross with me for staying longer, are you?'

'No, of course not. But something is wrong. Julia came over yesterday.'

'And?'

'Denis has walked out on her.'

Alan stared, the spoon halfway to his mouth.

'You must be joking.'

'Absolutely not.'

'When did this happen?'

Constance explained.

'The bastard! The absolute bloody bastard!'

This reaction, while it didn't exactly surprise Constance – Alan's judgements were usually swift and decided – also didn't reassure her. It was too emphatic, somehow, and too obvious. She said nothing.

'Did you find out who he's gone off with?' Alan asked.

Constance raised her eyebrows and said: 'I see that you immediately assume he's gone off with somebody.'

'Well . . . I wasn't aware of any discord between Denis and Julia. If he hasn't gone off with somebody else, it's even more mysterious.'

'Oh, he has. A girl. Twenty-four years old.'

'There you are. These girls don't miss a trick, some of them. Old Denis must be making twelve thousand a year.'

Constance again said nothing. Alan pushed the cornflakes aside.

'Amazing, isn't it?' he said. 'A really good marriage, years and years of happiness, and he's ready to chuck it away because some bird makes goo-goo eyes at him. I must say I thought Denis was more mature. My best friend. You never can tell.'

'I suppose you can't.'

'How's Julia taking it?'

'She was under control. But she's hard hit, naturally. Crushed, I should say.'

'I hope she doesn't give up too easily. It might turn out to be a passing attack of lunacy.'

'He's very stuck on this girl, from what he told Julia. It's been going on for over a year.'

'Is that so? The crafty old sod. I never noticed anything, did you, Connie?'

'No.'

'Still, he's only just left the happy home. He'll realise what he's losing, I shouldn't wonder. He's not a complete idiot. Tell you what, I'll have a talk with him. I'll give it to him straight, and no mistake. Where did he go?'

'To the girl's place, presumably. You would hardly expect Julia to ask for the address.'

'I'll call him at his office. I'll do it this morning.'

Alan looked at his watch, as though he expected Denis to be in his office at seven o'clock.

'You haven't had much breakfast,' Constance said.

'I don't feel like it. This has thrown me, it really has. I'll get dressed and take Prince out. I'll have rather a busy day if I'm going to see Denis as well as everything else.'

They stood up. Alan put his arm round her waist and caressed her.

'I'm sorry I wasn't here yesterday, darling. This must have been lousy for you. You've always been so close to Julia.'

'Worse for her.'

'Yes. Terrible. Terrible. OK, I'll get dressed.'

Alan was forty-eight, Denis was forty-eight, Constance was forty-six, Julia was forty-four. The friendship derived a special quality, and up to now a special strength, from the fact that the marriages constituted a foursome – the union of a male and a female twosome. Alan and Denis had known each other since the age of nineteen; Constance and Julia, being cousins, since childhood. The men first met in the Army, as corporals in a technical unit. Using their training, they got jobs in the same firm, and for a time they shared a flat. Alan then married Constance, who was a lab assistant. Denis moved out of the flat, but was a regular guest there. He felt himself to be a bit of a spare wheel; marriage, to judge by what he observed of it, seemed an excellent idea. At this point Julia arrived in London, having trained for the stage and done two seasons with a provincial rep. 'She'd do nicely for Denis,' Alan and Constance agreed. So it turned out.

Neither of the men saw themselves settling for a gradual ascent of the promotion ladder. Alan started a management consultancy and built it up by hard work and reliability. He advised on new processes and efficiency in general, and had clients in all the main industrial regions. Denis went in for making instructional films. His company, Bradeye, expanded by degrees into documentaries which were often shown on television. They had no unfulfilled ambitions, and saw themselves as successful self-made men. The families – three young Garrards, two young Bradleys – grew up in comfortable houses near the Heath, Victorian but thoroughly modernized.

As the children became teenagers, the mothers talked about finding work to keep themselves occupied. The trouble was that their careers were effectively over, rather than interrupted. Constance hadn't been highly trained in the first place and had long forgotten her scientific knowledge, even if it had been still relevant. Julia, after being away from the stage for so long, could scarcely expect worthwhile parts. After much discussion, and some rather humiliating unsuccessful applications, Julia got a job teaching English to foreigners and Constance as a doctor's receptionist. But after a couple of years they felt that their husbands were right in saying: 'You've proved your point, darling.' Both jobs involved awkward hours, including Saturday work when Alan and Denis wanted to go away for the weekend (country cottages were another badge of success); the work was routine, and of course the money wasn't needed and mostly went in tax. Life wasn't empty, anyway. They had plenty of friends, houses and gardens to look after, and in the Garrards' case a dog. It was quite a job, Constance used to say, being a lady of leisure.

The women met frequently – for morning coffee, or tea, or a shopping expedition, or to see a film if both husbands were out in the evening. The men also met at least once a week, usually for lunch as their offices were within walking distance. Sometimes they bumped into each other by chance at a party given by some big company. But the foursome, nowadays, gathered at longer intervals. There simply weren't many free evenings. Alan would sometimes say: 'Let's see if Denis and Julia can come over and play Monopoly tonight,' but it didn't always work out. Constance reflected that she hadn't seen Denis more than eight or ten times during the year since he had taken up with the girl, Terry. It hadn't been up to her to notice anything. If anyone ought to have guessed, it was Alan. But no doubt Denis didn't take the girl to a place where he might run across an old friend. Or perhaps it wasn't unusual in business circles for a married man to be having a drink with a girl. Constance really didn't know.

Alan phoned her during the morning to say that he'd been on to Denis's office, only to be told: 'Mr Bradley has had to go abroad at short notice.'

'Well, one can't do anything about that,' Constance said.

'No way. How about asking Julia over for this evening? I'd like her to feel she's got friends.'

'Right, I'll ring her.'

Julia was less composed than the day before, and broke down in tears during dinner. What affected her, presumably, was seeing Alan and Constance together in their home, in the same old secure way – and the three chairs round the table where there had so often been four. Constance had decided not to wear the new dress, but unfortunately wore black; as Julia was in black too and Alan was in an office suit, they looked like a family gathered for the reading of a will.

Julia told Alan everything she had told Constance, which still didn't throw much light on Denis's behaviour. Alan asked a number of questions – a little too relentlessly, Constance thought – mostly about the girl.

'Where did he meet her, to start with?'

'I've no idea.'

'Where does she work? I might be able to find out something about her.'

'I'm sorry, I don't know. I don't even know her surname.'

'He can't have been seeing so very much of her, if you didn't notice.'

'I wasn't keeping track of him. I never have. He was in Germany for a week not long ago. Or he said he went to Germany. That's the awful thing – I always assumed he was telling me the truth, but now I don't know.'

Alan pondered.

'Look, Julia, you shouldn't resign yourself to accepting that he's left you for good and all. You can imagine the girl saying: "Let's be honest, let's have it out in the open" – that sort of line. So he gets talked into it. It isn't necessarily what he wants to do. He doesn't know his own mind, that's my hunch. After a bit, he'll decide that all he wanted was to have a fling.'

'I didn't marry Denis for him to have flings.'

'Of course not. Still, you must admit he hasn't made a habit of it.'

9

'So far as I know.'

After this, there was no more to be said on the subject. Indeed, it was difficult to keep up a conversation. Everything that came to Alan's mind, or to Constance's, seemed to carry an allusion to their continuing happy marriage or to the memories of the foursome. Julia didn't want to play Monopoly. Guiltily, the Garrards were relieved when she went home.

At the end of the next week, they were due to go for their regular skiing holiday. Denis still hadn't surfaced. It seemed unkind to leave Julia alone; she had other friends, naturally, but not such intimate friends. Her daughter was at Keele and her son at Winchester. On Alan's advice, she hadn't told them what was happening. However, it wasn't clear what Alan and Constance could achieve by staying in London. Alan was a passionate skier and never missed his winter sports holiday. Business commitments made a postponement impossible. So off they went.

When they got back, Julia said that she had received a letter from Denis. He hated making her unhappy, he wrote, but it was best for them to know where they stood. He was sincerely in love with Terry and positive that he wanted to spend the rest of his life with her. He trusted that Julia would agree to a divorce. The letter was hand-written – at least he hadn't dictated it to his secretary – but was on office notepaper.

Alan rang up Denis and suggested lunch.

'Yes, old boy, I'll look forward to that,' Denis said in a hearty tone.

He was at the restaurant first, and waved cheerfully from their usual corner table.

'You look in great form, Alan. Don't tell me – you've been skiing.'

Alan thought that Denis too looked extremely well. He said so.

'I ought to look well. I've been to the Bahamas.'

'With your bird?'

Denis laughed. 'I assume that you've been following developments.'

'Naturally, we've talked to Julia,' Alan said.

'How is she?'

'Miserable. What d'you expect?'

'In an ideal world, nobody would ever get hurt,' Denis said. 'I've had my sleepless nights, I can tell you. I didn't take this decision easily. But one has to be honest, at the end of the day. I couldn't have faced myself if I'd gone on concealing the truth from Julia.'

The waiter hovered.

'Usual? A vodka martini for Mr Garrard and I'll have a Campari soda.'

'Julia told us about your letter,' Alan said. 'I shan't advise her to agree to a divorce.'

'I'm sorry to hear that. It doesn't alter the situation.'

'The situation is that you're having an affair. You've got a mistress. In fact, I gather that's been the situation for some time. The only new thing is that Julia has been informed.'

'Ah well, that just shows what a lot you don't realize. I don't blame you, mind. One has to be on the inside of this kind of experience to know what it means.'

'What do you imagine it to mean, then?'

'I don't imagine, I know. Put it like this.' Denis pressed the tips of his fingers together, as he did when outlining a film treatment to a sponsor. 'At a certain point in my life, I made a commitment to a woman which was absolutely irresistible, absolutely necessary for me as I then was. I've now made another commitment which is equally inevitable for me. This only happens once to some men. They're the lucky ones, I daresay. It's happened to me twice.'

'To date.'

'I'll ignore that,' Denis said generously. 'I'm only stating that the experience, commonly known as falling in love and easily recognized by those concerned, is as genuine now as it was on the previous occasion. I think I have a right to ask you to accept that.'

Alan said nothing. The waiter came for their orders.

'I'm going to have the pâté and a Dover sole. How about you, Alan?'

'I don't mind. I'll have the same.'

'That's it, then. And a bottle of Niersteiner.'

Alan drank his martini. He had an irritated feeling that the discussion, for which he had carefully prepared himself, was already over. Worse still, Denis had had the better of the argument – if it was an argument.

'Julia is your wife, at this point in time,' he said. 'She's devoted her life to you, she gave up her career for your sake, she's brought up your children. All she's ever asked in return is ordinary loyalty. Now you're proposing to give her the push just because you feel like a change. You wouldn't treat a secretary like that if she'd been satisfactory. It's not good enough, Denis.' This phrase struck Alan as weak, so he added: 'It's completely heartless. I'm sorry, but I feel bound to say that.'

'No offence taken, old boy,' Denis said, starting on the pâté. 'You had to say your piece. Connie and Julia are bosom pals, I'm well aware of that. However, it's also a fact that we're old friends. We've normally given each other credit for sincerity. On that basis, I'm sure we'll remain friends.'

'It won't be so easy.'

'I'd regret that very much. I'd like to tell you something, Alan. Terry is a very unusual young woman. She made it clear that she was willing to have a small corner of my life, to be my mistress, as you call it – anything. The only thing she couldn't do was to stop loving me. And I couldn't stop loving her. It was open to me to keep up the deceit as long as I liked. Only, it was a deceit. I was allowing Julia to believe that I loved her when I'd ceased to do so. I felt that, for the sake of what we once meant to each other, she deserved better than that. I didn't make my decision just to be happy with Terry, but also – above all – to be honest with Julia.'

'I'm sure that makes you feel very good. What Julia feels is another matter. You simply stated that you were leaving her, isn't that so?'

'If you mean that I didn't ask her whether she would prefer me to perform my conjugal duties while loving someone else, that's correct. I should have considered that suggestion . . . well, heartless.'

Alan felt, once again, outmanoeuvred. He asked: 'Where are you living?'

'In a rather appalling furnished flat, at the moment. I'll have to make other arrangements. The fact is, I'm run off my feet these days, and of course Terry's got her job, which means a lot to her. I suppose you know how things are, the budgets are so low I've got to make twice as many films to earn the same money.' Denis shifted the conversation deftly on to the topics they usually discussed at their lunches.

As they were putting on their coats, he said: 'Oh, by the way, you might tell Julia I've written to the children. I thought it was my responsibility.'

'How did they react?' Alan asked.

'Very sensibly. We've always brought them up to realize that their parents are human beings. Timothy says he's looking forward to meeting Terry, so I'm taking her down to Winchester on Sunday.'

Alan had promised to phone Constance after the lunch, but a rush of business calls made it impossible. He worked until seven o'clock, had a drink with a couple of his staff – actually three rounds of drinks, since there were three of them – and then couldn't find a taxi and had to go home by tube. Constance, with dinner spoiled, received his explanations rather curtly.

'How was Denis, then?'

'In the pink. He's had a holiday in the Bahamas.'

'I wasn't asking about his health. How did he behave?'

'Well...' Alan's main impression was that Denis seemed perfectly happy, at peace with himself and free from any sense of guilt. He didn't like to put it like that to Constance. He had remembered in the tube, too, that he had made no real attempt to persuade Denis to return to Julia.

'You could say that Denis is in a difficult position, at this point in time. He's obviously promised the girl that he's hitching up with her permanently.'

'Then he'll have to un-promise. She hasn't any rights in the matter.'

'She's a human being, Connie.'

'Of a sort.'

'Well, Denis really is very fond of her. I could tell that by the way talked about her. I'm afraid it's more than just a bit of skirt-chasing.'

'I suppose he took her to the Bahamas.'

'I imagine so.'

'It's disgusting.'

'I don't know that taking her to the Bahamas is more disgusting than living with her in London.'

'You don't? What d'you suppose a trip to the Bahamas costs?'

'Well, Denis earns the money, after all.'

'You're defending him.'

'Don't be illogical, honey. The way he's walked out on Julia is bloody awful. I told him so, very strongly. I'm just saying his going to the Bahamas is irrelevant.'

'Come on, let's eat,' Constance said.

They ate in silence for a few minutes. Then she said: 'You haven't exactly got good news for Julia, have you?'

'Julia's got to realize that it's a fairly serious attachment. There's no point in concealing the truth. Break it to her gently, of course. You know how to talk to her.'

'I rather think that's up to you, considering that you're the one who assured her that Denis would soon have, quote, had his fling, unquote. In any case, she's coming over tonight.'

'She is? Oh, Christ, that's a bit much. I've had a long day.'

'She knew you were seeing Denis, so it's only natural she'd want to hear about it.'

'OK, OK. When is she coming?'

'Any minute now. I didn't know you'd be back late, did I?'

When Julia arrived, Alan decided that she still looked too vulnerable to be given definitive bad news. He said: 'I'm afraid I didn't make a lot of headway with Denis. Maybe I couldn't expect to, just over a lunch.' He didn't mention either Denis's justifications or the holiday in the Bahamas.

Julia listened mournfully. 'They are living together, I suppose,' she said.

'I believe Denis mentioned something about being in a furnished flat.'

'Have you got the address? I don't like writing to his office.'

Alan didn't think she would gain much by writing at all, but he promised to get the address.

'I want to see him. As soon as possible.'

'Are you sure you want to, Julia? It might be painful for you.'

'That's for Julia to say, surely,' Constance put in.

'Of course it is. I'm just thinking, it might be a bit premature. He's in rather a . . . what you might call a state of euphoria about this . . . this new experience. Just at the moment, I mean.'

'You mean he's happy with her,' Julia said.

'Well, one assumes that being happy is part of having an affair, doesn't one? That is, until it works itself out.'

'I want to see him. I'm not saying it'll do any good. I just can't sit around . . . thinking of him . . . day after day. . . .' Again Julia was on the verge of tears.

'OK, I'll tell him,' Alan said hastily. He wondered how long it would take for Denis's tan to wear off.

Before Julia left, he remembered to say: 'Denis asked me to tell you he's written to Sarah and Timothy. He felt it was his responsibility.'

'What did they say?' Julia asked.

'I didn't go into that.'

Alan and Constance went to bed early. After Julia had gone, it didn't seem worth doing anything with the evening. Neither of them felt sleepy, however. He was aware of her lying tensely beside him, staring at the ceiling.

'Don't brood, darling,' he said. 'It doesn't help.'

She sighed. 'Alan, you don't believe Denis is going back to her, do you?'

'I'd say, not at present. Apart from anything else, he'd feel a bit of a fool . . . you know, chopping and changing.'

'How unpleasant for him.'

'It's unpleasant all round. One has to recognize that.'

'Except for this little tart. It's very pleasant for her, isn't it? In fact, she can't lose. If she hangs on to Denis, she's in clover. If not, she's quite young enough to move on to somebody else's husband.'

To his own surprise, Alan rebelled against the dismissal of Terry as a little tart. Denis wasn't, surely – any more than Alan himself – a man who went off with little tarts. Constance's picture seemed to miss the complexity, the possible depth, of what was happening.

'It's not necessarily that simple,' he said.

'How isn't it?'

'I've been thinking. Things like this don't happen out of the blue. There must have been something lacking in their marriage. Don't ask me what. But something.'

Constance turned on her side and moved her arm slowly across his chest.

'Could be,' she said. 'What would you mean by something lacking?'

'Ah, that's a deep question.'

'Darling.'

'Darling.'

As sometimes happened, Alan wasn't altogether in the mood to make love. However, he did.

A week later, he lunched with Denis again. This time they talked about business prospects, as they generally did. The personal 'situation' was at the back of Alan's mind, but he wasn't conscious of deliberately evading it. Denis certainly didn't evade it; casually, and as though it were entirely natural, he mentioned an incident involving Terry while they were on the subject of advertising.

Over coffee, Alan said: 'I forgot to ask you for your new address and phone number.'

'Oh, sure.' Denis wrote on a page of a memo pad. 'We're not quite up to entertaining. But come round for a drink, any time.'

'Thanks.'

'Terry's going to take a week off and go house-hunting when she can manage it.'

'You know,' Alan said, 'Julia wants to see you.'

'Oh, really?' Denis didn't seem at all put out. 'Well, that's fair enough, isn't it? I'll be glad to have a discussion with her, now the dust has settled a bit. I'll ring her up.'

'You ought to realize she wants you back.'

'In that case a discussion is obviously necessary.'

He rang up Julia and went to the house on Saturday afternoon. Alan and Constance were at their cottage for the weekend and didn't hear about the meeting until a few days later. Apparently, it was undramatic. Denis told Alan:

'I think she understands the way things are. Naturally, it's hard for her to accept. She isn't ready to do anything about a divorce. I'm not pressing that, of course. It doesn't make all that much difference in this day and age, even if Terry wanted kids, which she doesn't.'

Julia told Constance:

'It was strange, really. Seeing him sitting there, in his usual chair, it was as though all this hadn't happened. I didn't say most of the things I'd meant to say. Actually I didn't say much at all. I let him talk, and I thought: What absolute nonsense, it's just like a stupid telly play.'

After this, nothing happened for over a month. The men saw each other in town; the women saw each other in Hampstead. The cessation of the foursome left the twosomes to function as usual. Alan and Constance no longer discussed the 'situation', for there was nothing new to be said. Alan had ceased to think about the chances of the Bradley marriage being re-established. Like peace between Israel and the Arabs, it might come about, and of course it was desirable, but there was no sign of it. He wondered whether Constance had reached the same conclusion. Probably she had, but wouldn't admit it.

He didn't take Denis up on the invitation to a drink at the flat. Once he hesitated; he had dined with some Scottish industrialists at their hotel in Kensington, the party broke up early but Constance didn't expect him home until late, and he was a hundred yards from where Denis and Terry lived. He felt a keen curiosity, and a boyish sense of stepping on exciting forbidden ground. But he knew that Constance wouldn't approve, and the idea of going there and hiding it from her was too silly to consider.

Then, at a big party given by a telecommunications firm, he saw Denis across the room. They waved to each other. Denis was in a group, four men and two women.

Alan chatted with a few people he knew, and then found himself alone. Someone tapped him on the shoulder.

'Oh, hullo, Denis. I thought you were hemmed in.'

'I was trying to extricate Terry. Here she comes now.'

Terry said: 'You're Alan Garrard, aren't you? I'm so glad to meet you.'

The tone was just right: friendly, not too gushing, certainly not anxious – the tone of a new wife meeting an old friend of her husband's. Alan realized later, though he didn't formulate the thought at the time, that he had liked her once. He did think, as he shook hands, that she was far from what Constance and Julia imagined. She was attractive, certainly, but at all the glamorous siren type – less so than Julia had been at her age. She had auburn hair, cut quite short, alert dark eyes, and a neat but not sensational figure. In her sensible woollen dress, she looked like a young woman with a responsible job, confidently performed, and a satisfying but well-ordered private life. A man seen with such a young woman would be granted good sense and discriminating taste.

'Did you get your contract in Scotland, old boy?' Denis asked.

'Yes, that's all going according to plan.'

'Oh, that's good. How's Connie?'

'She's fine, thanks.'

Terry seemed content not to join in the conversation. After a few minutes, however, Denis was drawn away by a man in his line of business. Alan smiled at Terry: an inane, nervous smile, he was aware, which she returned calmly.

'Can I get you another drink?'

'No, thanks, I try and take it easy at these early parties. You have one.'

'I won't at the moment. I drink too much, anyway.'

'I'm sure that's not true.'

'Well, not alarmingly.'

She said: 'I'm working on a campaign for malt whisky. I'm thinking of: "When you feel like just one drink, but a real drink".'

'You know, that's very good.'

'I've also considered: "Feel plastered but beat the breathalyser".'

When she was claimed by someone else, Alan looked at his watch and found that they had been talking for twenty minutes. The time had passed easily and enjoyably – for him, at least; she might have found him dull. She had made several witty remarks and a thoughtful, well-informed comment on an article in the *Economist*. He was struck chiefly by what she hadn't said. Nothing predictable, such as 'Denis has told me so much about you'. She hadn't referred to Denis at all, nor to their relationship. Since Alan knew about it, it was to be taken for granted.

When he got home, Constance said: 'I took Prince to the vet. He's really in a bad way.'

'He doesn't look any worse than usual.'

'That's bad enough. He stinks. It's honestly rather revolting.'

Alan petted the dog. 'D'you stink, Prince? Poor old Prince. Can't help the way we stink, can we?'

'Oh, leave him alone, Alan, you'll stink too.'

'I'm sorry.'

'No, I'm sorry. I didn't mean to snap. Did you go to that party?'

'Yes.'

'Who was there?'

'Denis was there.' Alan paused. 'Also, Terry was there.'

'No! Well, that's a nerve, I must say.'

'Oh, come on, Connie. He can't keep her in purdah, can he? In fact, she may well have been invited on her own hook. It was full of advertising people.'

'Did you talk to her?'

'No. Denis tried to introduce us, but I said: "Strumpet! Scarlet woman! Get thee behind me, Satan!"'

'I don't find that particularly amusing.'

'Have a drink, Connie. Ease up.'

He poured the drinks. 'Thank you,' she said stiffly.

'Well,' he said, 'go on, ask me what she's like.'

'It's not necessary. I'm sure she's modest, charming, intelligent and well-mannered.'

Alan reflected that this was not a bad description. He said: 'I can see what Denis sees in her, at all events.'

'Oh, were you playing strip-poker?'

'Connie, for Christ's sake!'

'All right, I'm prejudiced, I know. I happen to be a woman. I'll try to see her from a man's point of view.'

'Look, darling, I've said a hundred times I don't approve of the way Denis walked out on Julia. It doesn't follow that Terry is devoid of good qualities. In fact, if she were, it wouldn't have happened.'

'I thought that, according to you, it happened because of Julia's bad qualities.'

'You're distorting my words. I said the marriage couldn't have been as solid as it looked.'

'Ah. I suppose that's the usual explanation.'

'What d'you mean by that?'

'It's a syndrome, isn't it? Men who've decided that being married just once is a bit tame; girls with a gift for coming along at the right moment. Denis hasn't been strikingly original.'

Alan thought this over. It was true that he could think of a number of examples, some within his personal knowledge and some reported in the newspapers.

He said: 'If you think it's so usual, why are you so het up about it?'

'Because I'm in a position to identify with Julia.'

'You're what?' Alan was genuinely startled. 'Let's be logical, darling. We don't know what was the weakness in their marriage, but we can guess there was one. Whereas we do know about our own marriage.'

'Yes,' she said slowly. 'We do, don't we?'

For a moment, something strangely vulnerable in her reminded him of Julia.

'Of course we do,' he said. 'This has been a bad jolt, I realize that.

Denis and Julia were our closest friends. But at the end of the day they're other people, and we're us. You mustn't let it affect you too much. Give me a kiss, honey.'

At Easter, the young Bradleys came home. They were something of a comfort to Julia, and she didn't know whether to be thankful or sad when she saw that they took the break-up of their parents' marriage as an event to which adjustment was entirely possible. Naturally they visited Denis at the flat, and naturally Terry was there. Sarah commented: 'She's quite bright and lively. Obviously she gives Dad delusions of juvenility.' Timothy said judiciously: 'She's definitely sexy.' Clearly, they assumed that Julia could only resign herself.

The Garrards, since their own children were also at home during the holidays, were temporarily out of touch with the Bradley 'situation'. Besides, Alan preferred not to talk about it. The crisis had been a strain for Constance – more than he'd realized until the scene after the party – and it was best kept out of her thoughts. Fortunately, as a crisis, it was over.

One evening in May, the phone rang when Alan was alone in the house. Constance had gone to spend a few days with her mother, who lived at Worthing and wasn't in very good health.

'Is that Alan?'

'Speaking.'

'This is Terry. How are you?'

'I'm fine. How are you?'

'Likewise. I'm ringing to say that we've managed to find a house at last. We've even acquired a few knives and forks, so we're hoping that you and Constance can come to dinner soon.'

'That sounds very nice. Constance is away just now, though.'

'Oh, will she be gone long?'

'No, no, only a couple of days.'

'In that case perhaps we can fix a date.'

She suggested one. Alan agreed to it, with the proviso that Constance might have made some arrangement. Terry gave the address and rang off.

When Constance was told, she said: 'Have we got to?'

'I left a get-out,' Alan said. 'But obviously if I say the date's no good they'll suggest another one.'

'I meant, at all.'

'We've always gone to dinner with Denis and Julia. Denis now lives with Terry. People do live together, you know, darling. It's no good being like Queen Victoria.'

'I've been waiting for you to say that. I can remember you being absolutely certain that Denis would go back to Julia.'

'Ah well, I did think that at one time. But it's about four months now. I don't suppose Julia herself expects to get him back. In fact, even at the beginning she was quite pessimistic – or realistic, as it's turned out.'

'All right, that may be realistic. It's another thing for us to behave as if we thought it was all perfectly splendid. When I think of the things you said about Denis! But I expect you've forgotten.'

'I haven't forgotten. I'm just saying that a point comes when it makes more sense to think in terms of a marriage having broken down, rather than of who was to blame. After all, even judges don't go in for that stuff about innocent parties and guilty parties nowadays.'

'I'm sorry, Alan, but I don't think I could bring myself to be polite. You go without me.'

'No way. You must see what that would look like.'

At the end of a confused argument, which centred more and more on the social difficulty of turning down an invitation which Alan had virtually accepted, Constance gave in.

The house was near Primrose Hill. It was small, as befitted a couple without children – a young couple, one was tempted to say – but charming, even elegant. Alan felt that his own house was sprawling by comparison; no doubt Denis felt the same about his former home. He wondered how Terry could have assembled a complete – and very tasteful – complement of furniture, pictures and household equipment at the same time as holding down a job. Decidedly, the house already had a lived-in feel. But perhaps it was Denis and Terry who created that atmosphere.

The other guests, presumably friends of Terry's, arrived late and explained that the delay was caused by their baby-sitter. This carried Alan back to a different, and in retrospect delightful, period of his life. The man was about thirty, he guessed, the wife a little younger. He was a psychiatrist. Placed beside the wife at dinner, Alan chatted to her on the assumption that marriage and children filled her time, until a question from Terry revealed that she wrote novels.

Over coffee and brandy, the conversation became general. It was mostly about new plays and films which everyone had seen except Alan and Constance. Even when he had seen one, Terry and her friends considered it from an angle that was new to him, and had noticed things in it which wouldn't have struck him. They were certainly clever people. Denis, whom Alan had never regarded as clever in this sense, seemed to be at ease with their vocabulary and their way of thinking. Alan was beginning to feel somewhat out of things, when Terry smoothly turned the conversation in a direction that helped him – though it didn't exclude the psychiatrist and the novelist, who were surprisingly articulate about the failings of British management.

Finally, after eleven o'clock, they talked about education.

'Do you have children?' the novelist asked Constance.

'Yes, but they're almost grown-up now,' Constance replied.

Alan realized that this was the first time he'd heard his wife's voice. Nor did he hear it again until they left.

He had time to reflect on the evening in the car going home, for Constance was still silent. There was no denying that Denis was happy with Terry and they were getting a lot out of life. All these new plays and films they managed to see, for instance. Alan himself liked an evening at the theatre. Denis had never gone much in the past, although Julia had been on the stage – or, it now occurred to Alan, because Julia had been on the stage and didn't want to be reminded of her abandoned career.

So far, he hadn't consciously compared the two women in his friend's life. But a comparison was inevitable now, for the dinner was on a Friday night and Julia came to lunch on the Saturday. This arrangement, made by Constance, wasn't much to Alan's liking; the weather was beautiful and he'd been hoping for a weekend at the cottage.

He had developed the theory that Denis and Julia had ceased to get anything out of sex. It wasn't much of an exaggeration to describe her as fat. Her complexion was poor, too, and she had deep crows' feet round her eyes. Constance, he confirmed with a glance, had crows' feet too. But Constance had an interesting face; he had always thought that, while being aware that she'd never been a beauty. One could well understand that a man would get tired of seeing Julia's face every day – those too rounded cheeks, those vague blue eyes. And those black dresses she always wore! Constance looked better in her customary sweaters and trousers, which at least varied in colour. Terry had worn a stunning dress last night, with gold-thread edging and a gold belt round her trim waist. Say what you like, a man appreciated that kind of thing. He was glad that Constance had looked well, in the new dress she'd bought just before the skiing holiday.

Letting his thoughts run on like this, he'd lost the thread of the conversation. Not that it was much of a conversation; Constance was explaining how to clear a blocked sink-disposal unit. Julia had always been useless at that kind of thing – it could well have got Denis down a bit, too.

Julia stayed all the afternoon. Alan was extremely bored. You had to face it, he thought – Julia was a boring woman. He took Prince for a long walk, right across the Heath.

That summer, he began to feel that Julia was in their house an awful lot. Constance always had a reason. If Alan came home in the afternoon, as he sometimes did to read reports without being distracted by the office phone, Julia was there. 'Well, I didn't know you'd be coming in,' Constance said. If he had dinner out with clients, Julia was there on his return. 'Well, you were out, so I didn't feel like being alone all evening,' Constance said.

The matter came out into the open when he and Constance were planning a dinner-party. 'It would be nice to ask Julia,' she said.

'Julia? Whatever for?'

'There's a spare man.' This was one of Alan's Scottish clients, spending a few days in London. 'And she knows Mike and Helen. I'm sure she'd enjoy it. She doesn't have much social life these days, poor Julia.'

'She sees plenty of us.'

'I always have seen Julia every few days. I don't propose to stop doing that in present circumstances.'

'No, no. Still, she didn't always stay so long.'

'She hasn't much to go home to. What are you trying to say, Alan? D'you object to having Julia here?'

'I'm not too keen on having her at this dinner, to tell you the truth. She doesn't exactly add to the gaiety of the occasion.'

'It's not her fault that she isn't bursting with happiness.'

'No, and it isn't other people's fault that her marriage has broken down. I don't see why she has to cast a gloom on the evening.'

'I see. Obviously you think that a deserted wife should be a social outcast.'

'I don't think anything of the sort. You're getting very fond of putting words into my mouth, Connie. I think she ought to do something for herself instead of always leaning on us. Why can't she get a job, for instance? That might cheer her up. She might even meet a man. She's still quite attractive, for her age.'

'What a charming remark. Julia is two years younger than me.'

Julia was invited to the dinner. She wore black and, in Alan's opinion, cast a gloom. Mike and Helen, who hadn't seen her since Denis had left her, seemed embarrassed. Alan didn't voice his impressions to Constance. He was preparing himself to suggest that it was time to reciprocate the evening with Denis and Terry, but he didn't relish the inevitable argument about this proposal.

He let it ride, though with a bad conscience. At the end of June, he and Constance went to Spain for their summer holiday. They had taken to going early; the children no longer came with them, but were likely to be at home in July or August in between hitch-hiking expeditions. Somehow, Alan didn't enjoy the holiday. Constance was happy sitting by the pool and reading thrillers, but he got bored. In the evenings, she seldom wanted to dance. She was a good dancer, but she was no longer keen on it. Sitting in the lounge, he gazed meditatively at younger couples who were chattering vivaciously – he and Constance didn't talk much – or slipping off to the bar or the dance-floor. The young men looked cheerful and self-confident, the girls all looked pretty. Most of them weren't married, he supposed.

Once, when Constance said she was tired and went to bed early, he got into conversation with a man who turned out to be an executive in a container company. Alan had done reports on containerization, so he looked forward to an interesting talk, even if it wasn't exactly what one went on holiday for. The man didn't belong to the young set; he was in good condition, in a sort of tennis-player way, but he was lined and white-haired and Alan judged him to be getting on for sixty. However, at about ten o'clock a delectable young woman, whom Alan had admired from a distance, came along and said: 'Where have you been, honey? I thought we were going to hit the town.' The man excused himself to Alan and went out with her. Second wife? Mistress? Secretary? Alan drank two large brandies on his own, but still felt gloomy.

Soon after the Garrards came home, Denis and Terry went on holiday. They travelled by car through Yugoslavia to Greece – but not to the coast or the islands. Terry wanted to explore the cliff-top monasteries in a district called the Meteora. They wore themselves out walking and climbing, evidently had a whale of a time, and came back with splendid photographs, taken by Terry. Alan knew that he would never have thought of anything so original and exciting. If he had, Constance wouldn't have been interested.

The Garrards always gave a big party in September, on or near Constance's birthday. A couple of evenings were spent enjoyably in drawing up the invitation list. Alan waited until the obvious names had been jotted down and then, with an appearance of casualness, said: 'Oh yes, Denis and Terry.'

'Oh no,' Constance said. 'We can't.'

'Why on earth not? You're not still doing your bit of ruling them out of the Royal Enclosure, are you?'

'We can't because Julia will be coming.'

'Oh, will she?'

'Yes, she will.'

'It's very awkward. Denis knows we give this big party for your birthday. He's always been there.'

'So has Julia. I refuse to have that girl here and shut my best friend out.'

Alan submitted; he was avoiding arguments with Constance these days. The party was a success, as usual, but he felt that it wasn't the same without Denis – his best friend. He also noticed, as he had never noticed before, how the years were leaving their mark on people he had known for a long time. The men were getting into the habit of swapping nostalgic memories; the women had lost their charm and their sense of fun; there was no one with whom he really enjoyed dancing.

He had avoided ringing up Denis during the last couple of weeks, but when Denis phoned he couldn't refuse a lunch.

'How've you been, then?' Denis asked when the waiter had taken their orders.

'Unbelievably busy, as a matter of fact,' Alan replied. 'I just go home and fall asleep in an armchair. Haven't been going out in the evenings, or seeing friends – just not up to it.'

Denis was silent for a minute. Then he said: 'You know, old boy, it'd be a poor do if we couldn't talk to each other frankly. I realize that Connie isn't ever going to be pals with Terry. Connie and Julia are family, they grew up together – you can't get over that, no way. And Terry grasps the situation. She doesn't resent it, she isn't that kind of girl. So why don't you come over for an evening now and then? We'd enjoy it – Terry really likes you – and I don't think Connie could object.'

'You know what?' Alan said. 'I think I'll take you up on that.'

He felt that the arrangement was ideal. It got him off the hook, and it would be a relief to Constance. He also felt grateful to Denis – and to Terry. They were the ones who were being generous and understanding.

He started going to Primrose Hill about once a week, sometimes for an hour just after work, sometimes for a whole evening when he'd been working late and had told Constance not to expect him for dinner, sometimes after returning from Wales or the Midlands. It was informal and simple; he had only to phone and find out if they were in. Naturally, he told Constance about it. She wasn't pleased, but she said: 'I can't stop you if that's what you want to do.' Having told Constance about the general principle, he didn't feel obliged to tell her about every single visit.

As often as not, there were other people in the little house. They dropped in, unexpectedly but always welcome; that seemed to be part of Denis and Terry's way of life. And sometimes they went to the pub, just a minute away. Since his young days, Alan hadn't been in the habit of going to a pub in the evening, as distinct from a bar near his office. There was usually someone in the pub whom Denis and Terry knew. It was that kind of neighbourhood, they told Alan.

The people whom Alan met in this way were mostly not in business. If they were, it was Denis's kind of business – 'the media' – or Terry's kind, advertising. Otherwise, they might be writers, artists, actors and actresses. Most of them were young. But if they were older, it didn't seem to matter. There was one writer, usually to be found in the pub, who was seventy-two – 'a hardy annual', Terry said, and Alan agreed. He wore a zip-up jacket, got a bit tipsy, and wisecracked with the barmaid, just like the young men.

The conversation was interesting, but what really attracted Alan was the atmosphere: always gay and lively, always easy and good-humoured. Because Denis and Terry were the fixed points as far as Alan was concerned, while other people came and went, he felt that they made this atmosphere – particularly Terry. Sometimes she did most of the talking, while Denis was content to listen. She was very much in the swim; it wasn't only the new plays and films she'd seen, but also her constantly replenished stock of anecdotes, gossip and rumours. She had an opinion on everything, though she didn't force it on anyone who disagreed. She was never tired, even if she'd just come in from work, and always ready to dash out to the off-license for a bottle or to dish up a meal for unexpected guests. And she had infected Denis with this youthful spontaneity, this freshness. No mistake about it, Alan thought, she'd done wonders for him.

He found that he was reluctant to leave Primrose Hill and go home. Constance seldom had any news, except that Prince had eczema again or that she'd waited in all day for the plumber and he hadn't turned up. Denis was lucky, Alan reflected, to have a wife (Terry was virtually a wife) who had an interesting job and came home with new stories to tell. Evenings with Constance, frankly, were not very exciting. They watched television, they read for a while, and they went to bed. Constance often seemed to be tired these days, though she had nothing to make her tired. She denied that she was tired, however – she was just relaxing, she said. Perhaps he imagined it; perhaps it was the contrast with Terry. He also noticed that what Constance had to tell him was usually a complaint, trivial in itself but magnified by the lack of other news. She was more often in a cross temper than she'd been in the past – or did he imagine that too? He couldn't, of course, expect her to be in a very amiable mood when she knew or guessed that he had been with Denis and Terry.

In November, Constance went to visit her mother. Normally she went for only a few days, but this time she said she would stay for a week. Alan would manage all right, she was sure. So he did. He came home after work, gave Prince a walk and supper, and went out again – either to see a film, or to see Denis and Terry. Somehow, he didn't miss Constance.

He had the custom of pausing in his work at four in the afternoon, when tea was brought in, and having a short sociable chat with his secretary. She was an intelligent girl, with a bright smile and a pleasant manner which made her popular in the office, and he liked her to get the idea that he didn't regard her as a machine. One day, when he had mentioned the film he'd seen the night before, she said that she was hoping to see the new play by Alan Ayckbourn.

'Well, can't your boy-friend take you?'

'Oh, plays aren't much in his line. Match of the Day is more what he goes for.'

'I'll take you if you like,' Alan said on impulse. 'I work you damn hard, you deserve a treat.'

'Oh . . . Do you want to see it yourself?'

'Yes, I'd like to. What about tomorrow night? You ring up for tickets. Your boy-friend won't object, will he?'

'He doesn't own me,' the girl said, smiling.

She went home to change while Alan saw to Prince. When he met her at the theatre, she looked like a different person; she wore her hair loose over her shoulders, instead of tied in a ribbon as at the office, and she had put on a low-cut blouse and a long skirt. He had been aware that she was nice-looking – he wouldn't have employed a secretary who was a frump – but now he realized that she was distinctly attractive. It was enjoyable to be with her, to catch appreciative glances in the theatre bar and when they returned to their seats. After the play, instead of taking her to a nearby pizza bar for a snack as he had intended, he gave her dinner at a good restaurant.

It was quite late by the time he drove her home. 'Thank you for a lovely evening,' she said with her brightest smile. He said: 'The pleasure was all mine,' and kissed her on the cheek. She had drunk more wine than she was used to, probably, and he had the feeling that a kiss on the lips would have been welcomed, and more wouldn't have been out of the question. Of course, he did nothing about it. She had a regular boy-friend and there was no sense in creating a difficult situation, nor in spoiling his normal easy relationship with her. But he drove back to Hampstead in a buoyant mood.

Constance came home with a string of complaints. The weather was worse on the coast than in London; her mother wasn't really fit to look after herself but obstinately refused to have a nurse; and it wasn't very nice to come back and find not a scrap of food in the house, so that she had to go straight out again to the shops.

'I'm sorry. I ate out mostly.'

'I see.'

Some days later, Constance said that she would like to see the new Alan Ayckbourn play. It struck Alan afterwards that it wouldn't have hurt him to sit through it twice. But this didn't occur to him at the time. He said: 'I saw it while you were away.'

'Really? Who did you go with?'

'I went by myself.' Why he said this, Alan wasn't sure.

She looked at him for a few seconds and said: 'It seems a funny thing to do, to go to the theatre by yourself.'

'Well, if you're away I can't just watch telly every evening, can I?'

To square his conscience, he took Constance to the opera, with an expensive dinner afterwards. The evening was not a success. He'd had a very busy day, and he fell asleep in the second act; he didn't really enjoy opera, though Constance did. Then, as he'd been obliged to skip lunch, he was desperately hungry by the time they got to the restaurant, and the service was poor. He barked at the waiter: 'Is the kitchen on strike or is it just a go-slow?'

'I wish you wouldn't behave like that,' Constance said. 'It's so embarrassing.'

'I don't see why I should put up with lousy service. It costs enough here, God knows. I don't come here to sit and twiddle my thumbs.'

'You could try talking to me, if only to pass the time.'

'I'm sorry. I'm not at my best. I've had a bad day.'

'Well, don't take it out on me.'

After they got home and went to bed, Alan couldn't sleep. The doze in the opera had left him wakeful and restless. He clicked on the bedside lamp to see his watch; it was a quarter past two.

Constance was fast asleep. Her high cheekbones, which he had admired when he first met her, had begun to give her face a rather drawn appearance. She had become thin . . . one couldn't say scraggy, but there wasn't much flesh on her. Better than fat, he supposed; a woman couldn't keep her figure for ever. In the past, they had always made love after a special evening out. Perhaps she had expected it tonight – he hadn't thought of it. He could wake her up. That had excited her once . . . in the past. She would only be annoyed if he woke her up now, probably. In any case, he felt no desire.

It was true that he'd been bad company at the restaurant. He was often bored when he was with Constance, he admitted to himself with the candour of night thoughts. After more than twenty years of life together, it wasn't easy to think of new things to say. She knew his opinions on practically every subject, and he knew hers. One couldn't expect the intriguing surprises, the sense of discovery, that came when one explored the mind and the feelings of a woman . . . of a person whom one was just getting to know. Actually, he couldn't remember when they had last talked in a way that brought them closer together, pouring out words, saying things that seemed fresh and significant. There could be no more of that. It was natural, just as it was natural that their sex life – though it was all right, of course – no longer had the power to bring them closer together than they were already. Natural: sad perhaps, but natural.

And yet. . . . He remembered a hot afternoon, a few months after they were married, when they both took a shower after playing tennis. He suddenly embraced her and tried to lead her to the bed, but she made him take her standing up. It gave her a special kick, and he recognized this as a secret of love. A woman, he reflected now, can offer this kind of secret as a man discovers her, but can offer no more secrets when knowledge is complete. They hadn't done it for years. Constance had doubtless forgotten about it, or wouldn't wish to be reminded of it, As he thought of it, Alan was seized by an almost unbearable sense of loss.

He slept badly and woke up early. It was only just light; winter was not far off. He tried to think with pleasure of Christmas, having the children at home, and then the skiing holiday. Somehow, none of these gave him the usual feeling of cheerful anticipation.

Constance stirred when she heard him getting dressed, but he told her to stay in bed. Nowadays, they didn't always have breakfast together. He decided to take the dog out and get down to the office early. He was lunching with Denis; if he got through a lot of work in the morning, they could make it a good long session.

The weather was nasty, so he cut the walk short. Prince didn't really need much exercise; when it was pouring, they only let him out into the garden and he was none the worse for it. He was showing his age. Alan wondered gloomily how long he would last. Constance wasn't fond of him – she wouldn't mind if he pegged out. She had been fond of Toby, the dog who had grown up with the children, and hadn't wanted another dog. Was it true that, without consciously realizing it, Alan had bought Prince so that there would be someone needing care and affection when the children became self-sufficient? If so, it hadn't worked out. Still, there would be an empty space without Prince.

Constance still hadn't come downstairs when he brought Prince back. He thought of going up to kiss her and tell her that he was sorry the evening hadn't been what it should have been. Leave it, he decided.

The lunch with Denis put him in a good frame of mind again. They lingered over brandy and cigars, comfortable in the knowledge that their secretaries were holding the fort. As they were settling the bill, Denis said: 'Oh, you might do me a favour.'

'Sure.'

'Actually it's a favour for Derek Callingham.' This was a BBC producer, a friend and neighbour of Denis's whom Alan had met three or four times. 'He's doing a programme on stainless steel. You know all about that, don't you?'

'Quite a bit. One of the companies is on my books, anyway.'

'D'you think he could send his researcher along to chat with you? Just a few guidelines.'

'Glad to help if I can. Tell Derek to contact me.'

The researcher, Derek said, was called Sheila Brooks. Alan gave her an appointment at five-thirty, when the phone calls would be easing up.

While he talked about tungsten and high-quality alloys she took notes earnestly but, he noticed, only on the more important points or when he gave her a fact that wasn't generally known. Apparently she had done some homework already. Her questions were intelligent, one might even say sharp.

'I've taken a lot of your time,' she said at six o'clock.

'That's all right. I'm finished for the day. I don't know why we're still sitting here, in fact. This is dry stuff, don't you think?'

'That's very true, Mr Garrard.'

They had to cross the street to the bar that Alan used. The girl stepped off the pavement in front of a car that was moving faster than she thought, and had to step back.

'Watch it,' Alan said. 'You've got a lot of life ahead of you.'

She gave him a quick self-mocking smile, took her spectacles out of her bag, and put them on.

'I'm dreadfully short-sighted really, only I hate to admit it.'

This little vanity amused him. She didn't need to worry about her looks, he thought. Her face was a perfectly proportioned oval, like a Spanish portrait. However, the glasses hid her fine brown eyes. She took them off when they were settled at a table in the bar.

'Have you been at the BBC long?' he asked.

'No, only a few months. Cheers, Mr Garrard.'

'Alan.'

'Right. I'm just finding my feet, I mean in these industrial subjects. A B.Sc.Econ. is one thing, and seeing the wheels go round is something else again.'

He wondered if she had just graduated. No, she had more poise and confidence than that; she must be about twenty-five. He asked: 'Anything in between?'

'I'm a working girl, Mr Alan Garrard.' She put the glasses on to prove this, then laughed and took them off again. 'I was with a development team in Kenya.'

'So you're also an idealist.'

'I'd say there are certain things I believe in. Or is that pompous?'

'Pompous wouldn't be among the adjectives I'd find for you.'

'Good. Nor you.'

Alan offered her a cigarette – she shook her head – and said: 'Kenya must have been exciting.'

'It was, very.'

'But enough was enough, I suppose?'

'No, that wasn't it. Something broke up, I mean on a personal level, so I wanted a change of scene.'

'I didn't mean to be inquisitive.'

'Not the adjective. Being interested in people is a good quality, isn't it? Anyway, I like talking about myself.'

'That's not a bad quality either.'

'Right. Let's just finish with steel, though. Could you tell me one or two people to see when I go up to Sheffield?'

'I might even be able to introduce you. I've got to go up there myself soon.'

'This does seem to be my lucky day.'

'I'm going on the twenty-third.'

32

'I hope that'll do for me. It depends on Derek.'

'Well, let me know. The BBC's not too bad on expenses, I hope. There's only one decent hotel.'

'Do you know, I like good hotels. I used to come into Nairobi once a month and stay at the Norfolk. It's a shameful taste, like Rémy-Martin, but I can't help it.'

'I'll do some research on whether they have Rémy-Martin here.'

Alan got home at half-past-eight. Constance said: 'You didn't tell tell me you'd be late.'

'I had to have a drink with somebody. It rather dragged on.'

Sheila phoned to say that she would be in Sheffield on the twenty-third. Alan wasn't in his office, so his secretary took the message. He completed the arrangements for his own meetings and inspections, and told Constance that he was going to Sheffield. She didn't ask whether he would be away one night or more. At one time, he thought, she would have asked that.

In the intervening days, he made a deliberate effort not to think about Sheila. When she did come into his mind, he found himself devising justifications. It wasn't his fault that the researcher was an attractive young woman. If she were a man, he would be giving just the same help to a friend of a friend. This was quite convincing, indeed quite true; so what was there to think about?

He took a morning train, checked in at the hotel, kept two appointments, and was back at the hotel soon after seven. The desk clerk said: 'There's a message for you, Mr Garrard.'

He took the piece of paper and, for some reason, hesitated before looking at it. But it was only a confirmation of an appointment for the next morning.

'Thanks,' he said. 'Oh, by the way, has a Miss Brooks arrived?'

'Just a minute, sir . . . Miss S. Brooks from the BBC? We have a booking for her, but she hasn't checked in yet.'

Alan went into the bar and bought a drink. After a few minutes, he carried the glass out to one of the tables in the entrance hall. He had some reports to go through; it didn't matter where he sat.

At a certain point during the next hour – while he was making notes on the reports, or reading the evening paper, or gazing at the doors to the street – he realized that it was desperately important to him whether Sheila arrived or not. This feeling was so strange, so much imposed on him without his choice, that it was almost frightening. Yet it was authentic and powerful, more so than any feeling he'd had for a long time.

He began to get the idea – though perhaps it was illusory – that the hotel staff were watching him inquisitively. In any case, he was behaving in a rather absurd fashion. He went into the dining-room and sat down at a small table.

While he was having dinner, Sheila came into the room. She was wearing a coat and evidently hadn't gone up to her bedroom yet. She peered round as best she could without her glasses. Alan almost burst out laughing.

He jumped up and hurried toward her. The space between them seemed enormous. She saw him, smiled and came to meet him.

'Hello,' she said.

SUCH A LOVELY GIRL

At the wedding, friends and relations kept coming up to Mrs Lambert and saying: 'You must be so happy, Mabel dear.' They also said: 'Such a lovely girl!' Mabel beamed, and sometimes dabbed her eyes. Her tears flowed readily at moments of emotion, even at the cinema.

She was indeed very happy. However, she was aware that when friends used the word, they meant 'relieved' too. The implication was fair. Jim was thirty; sometimes it had seemed that he would never get married. The modern idea was that early marriages were unwise, but Mabel didn't agree. Arthur had been twenty-two and she'd been nineteen, and they'd never had a moment of discord.

Jim had taken out – this was the phrase Mabel used, though she realized that more was involved – a bewildering number of girls. His parents met several of them, even after he left home and took a flat in London. The Lamberts had a big house on the edge of Epping Forest. Really it was too big; they hadn't expected Jim to be an only child. But it was a fine place to spend a Sunday, especially in summer – what with the large garden, the swimming-pool, and the Forest if you felt like a walk. So Jim used to bring his girls, or at least some of them.

Mabel suspected that Jim was teasing her; he knew that she would look at each girl and wonder: 'Is she going to be the one?' Her feelings, naturally enough, were mixed. On the one hand, she wanted to get Jim settled. Besides, having been disappointed in the hope of raising a large family, she hoped to have grandchildren before she was too old to enjoy them. On the other hand, the girl would have to be right for her handsome and clever son.

Though she was disposed to look for good qualities in people rather than faults, Mabel didn't find any of the girls ideal. One, although gorgeous to look at, hadn't a word to say for herself and was probably quite stupid. Another, on the contrary, was strident and argumentative. (A woman ought to have opinions but not to go about putting men right, Mabel thought.) A couple of the girls, she suspected, were out to make a good catch. Jim was an architect and obviously had a promising future. The girls probably imagined, too, that he came from a wealthy family. This was far from true; Arthur had worked hard all his life and had nothing but his salary as a mechanical engineer. The big house, the pool and the hi-fi were unintentionally deceptive. The house had been bought at 1930 prices and the mortgage long since paid off. The Lamberts had modest holidays, didn't give parties, didn't go to the theatre or dine in the West End except on their wedding anniversary, didn't even drink or smoke, so all their money went on well-considered, durable purchases. Mabel didn't omit to find ways of making this clear to the girls.

To complicate matters, there was an aspect of Jim's character that worried her. Much as she loved her son, she wasn't uncritically adoring. All these short-lived affairs – it was not only immoral (Arthur and Mabel had a firm code in such matters) but also selfish. She was afraid that Jim was turning into a Don Juan, taking his pleasure where he found it and heartlessly dropping girls when he was tired of them. One Sunday, when Jim had arrived with a girl but abruptly decided to go off and play golf with his father, Mabel found the girl weeping in the conservatory. 'Oh, Mrs Lambert, I love him so much and he doesn't seem to care!' On Jim's next visit, this girl had been replaced.

When Lorna appeared, therefore, Mabel kept her fingers crossed. Yet something told her that the prospects looked brighter than ever before. 'I believe he's serious this time,' she said to Arthur on Sunday evening. Arthur sipped his Ovaltine judiciously and said: 'He'll be a fool if he isn't.'

For one thing, as everyone said at the wedding, Lorna was such a lovely girl. All Jim's girls had been attractive, as one would expect, but Lorna was utterly beautiful – one of those creatures, as Mabel put it to herself, whom God makes now and then to show what He can do. Whether you looked at her graceful figure, or her luminous blue eyes, or the tresses of golden hair, you could only marvel at such perfection.

And, unlike some beautiful girls, she had a sweet nature. Without being shy or nervous, she was considerate of others – for instance, although she smoked, she didn't light up until they were in the garden, and then she carefully broke up her butts to avoid spoiling the lawn. She smiled readily, blushed prettily when Arthur paid her a compliment, and from time to time broke into a gay trill of laughter. Still, it was clear that she had a mind of her own. There was a firm set to her mouth that Mabel liked. She didn't contradict Jim when he said something she disagreed with, but she was likely to throw Mabel an amused glance to show that she wasn't convinced.

So Arthur and Mabel were willing, without reservations, to open their hearts to Lorna. Normally a reserved man, Arthur became quite animated when she came to the house, and delighted in showing her the collection of tin soldiers that he'd kept all his life. He rang up Jim in the middle of every week: 'You are coming on Sunday, aren't you? . . . No, no perhaps, we're counting on you . . . And Lorna, of course . . . That's grand, your mother's going to make a special dinner.' As for Mabel, even before anything was said about an engagement she found herself regarding Lorna as one of the family. To her gratification, Lorna took an immediate liking to the house – and in just the right way. She didn't remark on its size, nor praise the Lamberts' possessions as though assessing their value. 'It's such a comfortable house,' she said. 'So lived-in, so friendly. A real home.' And she made herself at home, starting with her second visit. 'I'll make the tea, Mrs Lambert,' she would say brightly. 'No, please let me – I know where everything's kept.'

The truth was, she told Mabel over the washing-up, that she'd never had a proper home, or not since her early childhood. Neither a home nor, sad to say, a family. Born in Kenya, where her father had a farm, she had been sent to a boarding-school in England just before the war began. Her father had been killed with the Eighth Army; her mother had remarried, and moved from Kenya to Rhodesia because of the Mau-mau. During school holidays, Lorna had lived with distant relations. She implied, without complaining or accusing, that she hadn't been happy. Now, she shared a flat with two other girls. 'It's all right,' she said, 'but there's only one sitting-room, we've each got our own friends . . . it's awkward sometimes.' Mabel's eyes filled with tears. If she'd had no other reason for wanting to see Jim and Lorna married, she would have wished it so that Lorna could have a home.

Lorna had a good job in the office of the *Architectural Review* – this was how Jim had met her – but she wasn't a career girl and she said, reassuringly for Mabel, that making a home was the hardest and the most worth-while kind of work. Though she didn't look it, she was twenty-seven. It was rather a puzzle that she was still single. Lucky for Jim, anyway.

The day came when Jim said proudly: 'We've got news for you,' and Lorna, smiling deliciously, held out her hand to show the engagement-ring. Mabel reached up to embrace her. (She was tall, while Mabel was short and dumpy.) Arthur said to Jim: 'You don't deserve her, my lad, but good luck all the same.'

When they settled down round the fire – it was September, but chilly – it seemed as though Lorna had always belonged there. 'I'm not losing a son, I'm gaining a daughter,' Mabel said. She added: 'As the saying goes,' for she realized that the phrase was far from original, but it expressed what she felt.

Since Lorna had no family, the Lamberts took charge of the wedding arrangements. The ceremony was at the old church in Epping Forest, the reception was at their house, and Arthur footed the bills. Champagne was served, of course; Arthur and Mabel had no rigid principles about alcoholic drink, they simply didn't enjoy it. Lorna didn't make much of a contribution to the guest-list – she didn't even ask her flat-mates, Mabel noticed – but what between Epping neighbours, Jim's friends, and Arthur's and Mabel's brothers, sisters, in-laws, nephews and nieces, the house was well filled.

After the honeymoon, the young couple returned to the house in Epping, to stay until they could find a new flat; Jim's little bachelor flat in Paddington wouldn't do for making a real home. The arrangement, as a temporary arrangement, was very sensible. Jim's old playroom could be used as a sitting-room if they didn't want to spend every evening with his parents. It was true that Jim had a long journey to work, but Arthur had been making the journey for years and years. Father and son drove to the station together, reminding Mabel of the old days when Arthur had dropped Jim at school. Lorna had given up her job to concentrate on flat-hunting. She didn't go into London for this purpose every day; it was no fun trailing round in the rain, nor in the cold spell which came early that year. Mabel used to say: 'Don't bother about it today, dear – there's no hurry, is there?' She was delighted to have Lorna in the house. They worked together on household tasks, and what with lunch and tea, and a walk down to the local shops, and spells of just sitting and chatting, the day went fast and they were both surprised when it was time for the men to come home.

Mabel felt that she was really getting to know her new 'daughter', and the more she knew, the more she liked her. Lorna wasn't in the least the kind of modern young woman whom Mabel found daunting. She was always ready for a chat about simple everyday matters, for although she was certainly intelligent, and could bring you up short with a sharp remark from time to time, she didn't set up to be an intellectual. Jim sometimes tried to get her to read heavy books, but she told Mabel with a laugh that she skipped through just enough to pretend. Her political views – not that she cared much about politics – were based on sound common-sense, without any of the high-faluting idealism that was in vogue with most of Jim's friends. It was the autumn of the Suez crisis; Lorna agreed with Arthur and Mabel that Britain should have finished the job and taught Nasser a lesson, and only Jim got worked up about the UN and international law. Lorna also considered that it was ridiculous to thrust elections and self-government on primitive natives, and on this point nobody could contradict her since she'd been brought up in Kenya.

But politics came up only when the men were at home. During the day, Mabel nodded approvingly while Lorna expressed opinions like these:

'All this modern art is just a swindle, if you ask me. I like to look at a picture and know what it's a picture of.'

'I think there's too much these days of letting kids run around and do what they like. It wouldn't do them any harm to learn proper manners.'

'It's getting too much, this sex, sex, sex all the time. People would be happier if they didn't think about it such a lot.'

This last opinion of Lorna's, though Mabel endorsed it as a general statement, did sound a bit surprising from a newly married young woman. Jim and Lorna were in love – that went without saying – and Mabel believed that sex had a rightful place as an expression of love between husband and wife. In the early days of her own marriage she had thought about it a good deal, very happily and without shame, while waiting for Arthur to come in from work. But she hadn't talked about it to her mother, let alone Arthur's mother, so she didn't try to pursue the subject with Lorna.

Having Jim and Lorna in the house – or 'at home', as Mabel put it – involved a few adjustments. Sherry was kept in the lounge, as the young people liked a glass before supper, or dinner as it was now called. Ashtrays also appeared; Mabel told Lorna to smoke when she felt like it, and she did smoke rather a lot. When she went into town, Mabel gave the house a good airing. But this was a small price to pay for the pleasure of her company.

The temporary arrangement lasted for over two months. It wasn't easy to find the new flat, and then Mabel pressed Jim and Lorna to stay over Christmas and New Year. 'It does seem quiet, all on our own again,' she said after they'd gone. They still came for weekends, however, and Mabel went several times to help Lorna settle into the flat. It was a nice flat, Mabel thought, in a big old-fashioned block near Maida Vale. 'It's not very nice looking out on that depressing courtyard,' Lorna said. She had wanted a flat facing the tree-lined street, but Jim said they couldn't afford it. The flat would do, Lorna concluded, until Jim was earning enough to buy a house.

Soon there was good news again: Lorna was pregnant. The baby was expected in October, just a year after the marriage. It was a very hot summer – baking, Lorna said, in the flat. She and Jim spent every weekend at the house in Epping, and then she stayed for the whole of August; she didn't want a holiday, so Jim went walking in Scotland with a friend. The Lamberts willingly put off their own holiday. Mabel didn't let Lorna help in the house, and she was content to sit in a shady spot in the garden, idly thumbing through magazines. She found the pregnancy a trial, partly because of the hot weather, perhaps also because she disliked 'looking like an elephant', as she said, and wasn't sure if she would get her perfect figure back again. She was, in fact, enormous. At the clinic, she was told to be prepared for twins. Genetically, this was not astonishing; Arthur's elder brothers were twins.

'I wish I could look forward to it more,' Lorna said. 'It's the thought of that hospital that gets me down. Grim old place – should have been pulled down ages ago. And I'm sure it's dirty. And those beastly black nurses.'

'Why don't you have it in Epping?' Mabel suggested. 'There's ever such a nice hospital. Quite small, you know, and friendly. I'm sure you'd be happier in there.'

'Oh, Mother, could I?'

It was the ideal solution, obviously. Lorna would get visits from Mabel in the afternoons, and when she came out of hospital she would stay at the Lamberts' house for a few weeks. It would be nice for her to have Mabel's help in coping with her first baby – or babies.

Mabel was very glad she'd made the suggestion. Lorna did have twins: two sweet little boys, and perfectly healthy. But it was a difficult birth, and left Lorna exhausted. The period after the birth was difficult too. Lorna didn't have enough milk to feed both babies, and they had to be coaxed to use the bottle, a task at which their grandmother showed more patience than their mother. One or other of them cried half the night, so Mabel was thankful that she was there to look after them in the daytime and let Lorna get some rest. The few weeks lengthened into another two-month stay.

'We really can't impose on you any longer,' Lorna said more than once.

'Impose on us – whatever d'you mean?' Mabel answered. 'This will always be home for you, dear, and don't you forget it.'

But Jim said to Arthur: 'Lorna's got to get used to coping with the kids in the flat sooner or later, and the longer she puts it off the harder she'll find it.' Besides, he'd be able to get home sooner; his office was only a short bus ride from Maida Vale. So Lorna, not without visible regret, packed up the innumerable odds and ends that go with a woman and two infants.

Four years went by before the next big event in the Lambert family.

The twins – David and Jonathan – grew more adorable every time Arthur and Mabel saw them. They were dark-haired and brown-eyed, taking after Jim; and they were so alike that even Lorna couldn't tell them apart, and had to sew D's and J's on their clothes. Mabel decided that David had the more loving character, while Jonathan was going to be the clever one. However, there wasn't much in it – both talked, and learned to do things like building card-houses, at an early age, stimulating each other as they grew up together. It was a joy to see Lorna playing in the garden or splashing in the pool with them. Her figure was still perfect, and although she creamed and powdered her face more carefully when she was past thirty, she was still what she'd been – a lovely girl.

But she didn't have any more children. The twins were quite enough of a handful, she said. And what if she had twins again, or maybe triplets? – no, thanks very much. She was a good mother, one couldn't say anything to the contrary, but she did tend to regard kids as a task rather than a blessing. She would play with them for ten minutes or so, and then say abruptly: 'Right, now you can carry on by yourselves.' When they were noisy or disobedient, she slapped them hard enough to hurt. Mabel sometimes intervened on their behalf: 'They're only little tots, dear, after all.' Jim, too, thought that Lorna was too strict. But Jim worked very hard and didn't see much of his children.

So the twins, naturally enough, were very attached to their grandparents. Arthur used to take one of them on each knee and read aloud, in a grave unhurried manner, from books left over from Jim's childhood. They loved these old books, such as *Winnie the Pooh* and the Beatrix Potter stories; Lorna didn't buy them many books, apparently. Sometimes, too, Arthur got out all his tin soldiers and showed the boys how to line them up in parade-ground order. As for Mabel, she didn't care how long she spent playing on the floor with them with Jim's old set of wooden blocks. 'I believe you're enjoying it more than they are,' Lorna said.

Jim and Lorna and the twins – or Lorna and the twins, when Jim had to catch up with work – came to Epping almost every weekend. 'Go to Granny's house!' the boys learned to demand as soon as they could talk. They also came for a month in the summer, usually in June when the weather and the garden were at their best. Jim came the first year, but after that he stayed in the flat. The twins took over the playroom and made it into a regular old glory-hole; Lorna instructed them to put everything away before bedtime, but Mabel said she didn't mind tidying up. It was generally Mabel who bathed them and gave them their supper. Lorna deserved a rest, she insisted. On top of this, Arthur and Mabel took the twins for a fortnight in August while Jim and Lorna had a holiday.

'You're a heroine, really,' Mabel's friends told her.

'Oh no, I don't mind a bit. It isn't a proper holiday, is it, if you've got to look after kids. Mind you, Arthur and I always took Jim with us when he was little. But we hadn't any choice. Anyway, I think it would be a trial for Lorna, keeping them amused in hotels and all that. So it's best for all concerned. And they're so happy here.'

It was wonderful, indeed, to see how carefree and contented the twins became at Granny's house. The flat wasn't very big, of course; there was no garden and they weren't allowed to play in the court-yard because there were some rough children. It wasn't really a good place to bring up a family, Mabel thought. She went to the flat now and then to baby-sit and stay the night (on a divan in the living-room). Jim and Lorna didn't know many of their neighbours – flats are like that – and had trouble getting baby-sitters. Although she didn't like to say it, even to Arthur, Mabel sensed that the twins were glad when their parents went out and they were left with her. 'Can we play a game?' they would ask, as if this were a rare treat. Lorna was often tired by the end of the day, and Jim liked to sit down and read a serious book. Actually, there wasn't much in the flat to play with. Mabel generally brought something from 'home' that the twins liked. The flat was rather bare altogether: no pictures, no ornaments, very few of the odd possessions that most couples collect as time passes. It was almost as though Jim and Lorna didn't see it as their home.

When she went to the flat, Mabel also felt – she didn't quite know how to put this, even to herself – that the marriage wasn't quite the kind of marriage that she'd had from the start with Arthur. In some respects, Jim and Lorna lived separate lives. For instance, when a name came up and Mabel asked: 'Who's that?', Jim would say: 'Oh, she's a friend of Lorna's' – or else Lorna would say: 'One of Jim's pals, I don't know him.'

'It sounds peculiar,' Mabel commented to Arthur.

'Well,' he said, 'it stands to reason they each had their own friends before they met each other.'

'Yes, but you make new friends together when you get married, don't you? At least, we did.'

'Things have changed,' Arthur said. It was his usual way of closing any discussion about Jim and Lorna; he was, by principle and inclination, reluctant to make judgements.

By degrees, Mabel made up her mind that Jim was behaving rather thoughtlessly. Lorna wasn't the sort to complain, but now and then she dropped a few wry remarks which revealed that she had a lot to put up with. While she was living as a wife – necessarily, with the housekeeping and the kids – Jim hadn't shed his bachelor habits. In spite of living so near his office, he often didn't come home until the twins were in bed. It might be on account of extra work, but more likely it was a matter of adjourning for a drink. When he did come home, he sometimes ate a quick meal and went out again, to the pub in Paddington which had been his local before he was married. That, apparently, was the advantage for him of living in town, instead of in a nice house in the suburbs as Lorna would have preferred. He took her to a film or a show occasionally, but there were many evenings when she was left alone with the television.

As well as this, he had got involved in politics. He was active in the Labour Party and the Campaign for Nuclear Disarmament and kept going to meetings. He even pushed off every Easter on the Aldermaston march. You couldn't expect Lorna to be very pleased about that.

There were a lot of political arguments even at Epping, to say nothing of what Mabel had to imagine at the flat. Jim held forth relentlessly about H-bomb tests causing cancer and defective children – not very pleasant for a young mother to have to listen to. Lorna's point of view was simple and, as Arthur and Mabel thought, sensible: the country had to be defended.

'But there isn't any defence. That's what I'm trying to tell you.'

'I suppose you'd have caved in to Hitler in 1940.'

'There weren't any H-bombs in 1940.'

It usually ended with Jim saying in a tone of controlled exasperation: 'If you prefer not to face facts, that's your business' or 'You just don't want to understand.' Lorna tightened her mouth; what she would have said if they'd been alone, Mabel could only guess. While she was sure that Lorna was right, what she chiefly felt was that political arguments between husband and wife were unseemly, and moreover a bad sign. Since Lorna didn't really care about

44

politics, the angry tone of these arguments showed that there were other disputes on more personal matters.

Mabel and Arthur were not present at these disputes – rows, perhaps? – but occasional confidences from Lorna told Mabel what they were about.

The children: Jim wanted Lorna to let them scamper about in the courtyard, or at the Council's adventure playground or even on bomb-sites, like other kids in the neighbourhood. They hadn't any freedom and they hadn't any friends, he kept complaining. Lorna said it was better than having the wrong sort of friends. Jim then accused her of being snobbish – and racialist, since some of the local kids were black.

Money: Jim nagged at Lorna for being extravagant. She did insist on their having a roomy, comfortable car; she liked to stay at a good hotel on holiday; she was particular about her appearance and bought good clothes. Jim seemed to think that such things didn't matter. If he'd had his way, he would have lived like a student – going about in old sweaters, hitch-hiking and camping on holiday – and made Lorna do the same.

Money again, on the income side. Jim worked for the Paddington Borough Council, and Lorna wanted him to go into private practice. Some architects of his age were coining it, working on office blocks and hotels for wealthy clients, while others were becoming famous for the modern houses they designed for celebrities. But Jim stuck obstinately to what he called 'useful work', building dreary blocks of flats for Council tenants. He wasn't so young any more – nor was Lorna. Allowing for the value of money, he was earning less than Arthur had at the same age, and Arthur had started from nowhere. At this rate, Lorna hadn't much hope of ever living in a nice house or bringing up the twins in a suitable environment.

Mabel and Arthur, especially Mabel, sympathized with Lorna on every count. Perhaps she was a bit too strict with the boys, but Jim's ideas were ridiculous, and he didn't devote much time to being a father anyway. It wasn't Jim who would have to wash and mend their clothes, or rescue them if they were bullied, possibly injured. Then, it was unfair of him to criticize Lorna's spending while he wasted money in pubs, especially when he didn't earn enough in the first place. And a wife had a right to expect her man to get on in the world. She could have had her pick of husbands, after all; in bestowing her lovely self on Jim, she had deserved more than what she was getting. Sometimes Mabel thought that Jim's cranky 'progressive' ideas were the cause of the trouble, but it was truer to see them as another symptom. She felt sadly that all his faults were coming out: his irresponsibility, his obstinate indifference to normal standards, his selfishness. Could it be that her son wasn't cut out to be a proper husband?

A time came when it was no longer fun to have Jim and Lorna at Epping. The tension began when they got out of the car with forced smiles, and there was always the danger that the most innocent question might spark a smouldering quarrel into flame. Lorna always looked tired, while Jim looked bored and resentful, obviously wishing to be somewhere else. In fact, although it was an awful thing to think of, Lorna seemed happy only when she came without Jim. In June, she regained the capacity to relax and laugh, like the children. Of course, she loved the house.

'She won't put up with it for ever, mark my words,' Mabel said to Arthur.

He shuffled uneasily in his chair, as he did when confronted with unpleasant facts, and said: 'Can't do much else, can she?'

'That's what I'm wondering.'

'What d'you mean, dear?'

But Mabel didn't put what she meant into words. Instead, she said: 'You'll have to talk to Jim, Arthur.'

'What about?'

'Well, about getting into this private work, for one thing.'

'All right, I will.'

He didn't. It was never any use telling people what they ought to do, he believed.

When Mabel thought of what it would be like if Lorna left Jim, she had to sit down for a quiet cry. She had so much to lose – the lovely girl whom she'd taken as a daughter, the dear little boys, the happy summer days. Surely it couldn't happen.

It did happen, though not exactly as Mabel feared. One winter day, a letter came from Jim.

'Dear Mum and Dad,

'I'm afraid this letter will be a shock for you, but you'll have to know, and perhaps it won't be altogether unexpected. Lorna and I have decided to separate. There are all kinds of reasons, but it's enough to say that we can't be happy together and I realize that I should never have asked her to marry me. She will of course have the flat, as well as the car and other possessions, and the children are with her pending final arrangements. I am staying with friends at the above address.'

Arthur had gone to work. Mabel had a cry, then put on a warm coat and hurried off to the station. Lorna was at home – she was nearly always at home.

She was calm, bravely and (Mabel felt) almost unnaturally calm. When Mabel seized her hands, she freed them and said: 'Would you like some tea, Mother?'

'Sweet of you, dear. Don't you trouble, I'll make it.'

'All right.'

Mabel filled a kettle.

'Tell me everything, dear. It helps to talk about it. Did you have a row?'

'We did, but that's nothing new. He said he wished he'd never met me, and he wasn't prepared to keep up the pretence any longer. There's not much to say after that, is there?'

'You'll make it up, Lorna.'

'I wish I believed that. Jim doesn't often change his mind.'

The twins, hearing their grandmother's voice, ran in from their room. Mabel dabbed her eyes.

'Poor little things.'

'They'll survive,' Lorna said crisply.

Mabel cooked lunch and stayed all day, playing with the children. Lorna said: 'Do you mind if I leave them with you? I've hardly been out of this bloody flat for three days.' She went to the cinema. When she came back, Mabel said:

'I've been thinking, dear. It must be awful for you here, all alone with the boys. Why don't you come home with me? Stay for a bit, just to get over it and sort yourself out.'

'Oh, bless you, Mother. I must say a change of scene would be welcome.'

Lorna packed two large suitcases. Tramping across the courtyard to the car, they were watched by several curious neighbours. Lorna ignored them; there was no one she wanted to say goodbye to.

Arthur, warned by phone, was ready with hot soup. He kissed Lorna gravely and said: 'I'm sorry about this, I really am.'

'These things happen,' Lorna said.

'I'm glad Mother thought to bring you out here, that's all. You've always liked this house, haven't you?'

'Yes, indeed.'

After two days, Arthur and Mabel realized that Jim's letter hadn't been answered. He was their son; they couldn't pretend that he didn't exist. Reluctantly, Arthur phoned him at his office and arranged to go and see him on Sunday – at the flat, since no other place came to mind. It was an uncomfortable interview, in every sense. Lorna had switched off the heating.

'Well, I hope you're pleased with yourself, son,' Arthur said.

'No, I'm not pleased. But I'm not sorry either. I've put an end to an intolerable situation. I'm relieved, to be precise. I'm sure Lorna is, too.'

'Is there any chance you can pick up the pieces?'

'None whatever.'

'You won't find anyone else like Lorna, you know.'

'I'll be very careful not to.'

Arthur fidgeted with a button of his overcoat and said: 'Now then, it doesn't do any good talking like that. You were happy with Lorna before things went wrong.'

'So I imagined. It wasn't much of a reality. Look, Dad, Lorna and I are simply incompatible. There are many reasons, as I said in my letter. D'you want me to go into details?'

'No, no,' Arthur said hastily. 'You could have made a go of it, all the same. You didn't treat her right, I've got to say that.'

Jim shrugged, lit a cigarette, and dropped the match on the floor, as if he were in a derelict house.

'Sorry's not such a big word,' Arthur said. 'You can still get her back if you try.'

'I don't want to. Please accept that, Dad.'

'I hope there isn't a reason you don't want to.'

'If that means what I expect, you're right. Yes, I've got a girl. She isn't the cause of what's happened, but she's important to me.'

'I'm sorry you can sit there and say that, Jim.'

'Christ, I'm due for a bit of happiness, don't you think?'

Set against Jim's surly defiance, Lorna presented a picture of touching dignity. Even now, she didn't speak bitterly of Jim; she simply never mentioned his name, unless Arthur or Mabel did.

When she was asked if she could ever agree to make it up with him, she said: 'If he's got anything to say, I'll listen.' It was for him to make the first move, of course – she didn't propose to beg him to come back. But there she was obviously justified, since the blame was entirely on Jim's side. Mabel hated having to say this about her own son, but it was no more than the truth.

Meanwhile, Lorna was at peace and clearly glad to be in the Lamberts' much-loved house. David and Jonathan were delighted to be there, too; they didn't seem to miss their father and certainly didn't miss the flat. In fact, it was just like the annual visit except that it was winter. Christmas wasn't far away, so Mabel got the twins involved in helping to decorate the house.

After a few weeks, Arthur and Mabel agreed that Lorna had made a remarkable recovery. She laughed and chatted easily, she never seemed to give a thought to the past. Apparently she had written off the collapse of the marriage – or the marriage itself – as an experience best forgotten. No doubt she had foreseen the break-up and prepared herself for it; she had guessed that Jim was unfaithful, she mentioned. Arthur and Mabel could only admire her. She had plenty of inner strength, that was certain.

A letter came from a solicitor, acting for Jim. If Lorna wished to sue for divorce, the petition would be uncontested. The solicitor also asked whether she wanted the tenancy of the flat transferred to her name. It was implied that Jim didn't see the sense of paying the rent for an empty flat. He had a new flat of his own, where presumably he was living with his girl.

'I couldn't go back to that flat,' Lorna said decidedly. 'I've been so miserable there. I never liked it, anyway.'

'You know you're welcome here as long as you feel like staying,' Mabel said. 'Arthur'll help you fetch the rest of your things.'

'You're so good to me, Mother.'

'Nonsense, dear, it's a joy to have you.'

So the house at Epping became Lorna's home. Provisionally, of course; the Lamberts assumed that she would want a place of her own sooner or later. But the house was big enough to make her comfortable for as long as necessary. She had a large bedroom, so did the twins, and they had the playroom.

True, Arthur and Mabel had to get used to certain changes. Lorna brought some furniture from the flat – not much, just a few chairs and an antique Welsh dresser that she was attached to, but enough to make the lounge look rather crowded. There had to be a television set, which the Lamberts had never wanted. It was on a great deal, first for children's programmes, then most of the evening; Arthur had to endure a lot of thrillers and comedy serials when he would rather have read a book or played his favourite records. Then, the lounge was always full of smoke. Lorna smoked heavily these days, doubtless because of the strain she'd been under, and it was rather a nuisance in winter when you couldn't keep the windows open. Then again, Arthur didn't really like watching her drink – always a couple of gin and tonics before dinner and whisky afterwards. Sometimes Arthur and Mabel left her with the whisky and the TV and went into the front room. This was the name for a second reception room which had never been much used, except for Jim to bring friends home during his teens.

And, much as Mabel loved the twins, she found that they were a bit rowdy at times. The noise gave her headaches – though whether it was the children's noise, or Lorna shouting at them, she wasn't sure. They were of an age when they needed friends to play with, and quite ready to start school, but the local primary school wouldn't take them until they were five, and that wouldn't be until the autumn. Luckily Lorna found a private school which was glad to have them. That ensured peace in the house, at least till mid-afternoon. Mabel gave them their breakfast and Arthur took them to school on his way to the station; Lorna wasn't much of a one for getting up early.

Looking back later, Arthur and Mabel couldn't place the exact time when they recognized that Lorna and the boys would be with them for good. Perhaps it was when she decided to keep the boys on at school where they'd started and remarked that another upheaval would be bad for them; perhaps it was when she began making friends in the district; perhaps it was when she joined the local Conservative Association. Nothing was explicitly said. If she didn't feel the need for a place of her own, they were reluctant to raise the matter or even drop hints.

It was unusual, one had to admit, for a woman to live with the parents of her ex-husband. (The divorce went through smoothly.) For a time, even after they'd ceased to believe it themselves, the Lamberts told their friends that she was looking for a house. However, when this fiction was allowed to fade out, people in Epping didn't seem to find the situation too extraordinary. They grasped that Jim had been to blame, that Lorna had no family of her own, and that Mabel adored the grandchildren.

Jim married his girl, who was called Maggie. Arthur and Mabel didn't go to the wedding – it was quiet, at a registry office of course – but when Jim invited them to a Sunday lunch they felt that it would be right to accept. Maggie wasn't a patch on Lorna, but she was quite pretty. She was an architect too, she was evidently the intellectual type, and she shared his political views. So she was right for him, it was to be hoped.

He had a right to see the children one Sunday a month, and for a week in summer. Lorna made herself scarce on these Sundays; Jim – sometimes with Maggie, sometimes not – came in for a chat with his parents before taking the boys to the seaside or whatever. They didn't think much about these outings beforehand (which was just as well, because Jim didn't use all his Sundays) but seemed to enjoy them well enough. In summer, he took them camping for a week, and they did look forward to that.

Jim's second marriage proved to be a success. After a time, Maggie had children. Mabel was surprised; Maggie had struck her as very much a career girl and Jim as a reluctant father. But there they were, the children – a girl, then a boy, then another girl. Mabel would have liked to get to know her new grandchildren, but didn't get much chance. Soon after the second child was born, Jim got a job as architect of a New Town in Lancashire. Maggie had always been civil enough to Mabel, but probably considered her a bore and didn't invite her to visit. Mabel punctiliously sent birthday and Christmas presents to grandchildren who wouldn't have recognized her. Jim no longer saw David and Jonathan on Sundays, of course, though he still took them for the week's camping. To his parents, he had become more like a nephew than a son – a man with a world of his own, with a little-known wife and family, whom they saw at long intervals. He grew a beard, he started to wear spectacles; Lorna probably wouldn't have known him if she'd seen him.

Lorna and the twins were Mabel's real family. As the years went by, they became more deeply attached to the house – to their home. Actually, even if Lorna had wanted to move she wouldn't have been able to afford to. Jim didn't send her any more money than he was obliged to; his new job carried a better salary, but by that time he and Maggie had a growing family. Lorna had to meet the school fees; she kept up and replaced her car; she had holidays abroad, sometimes taking the twins along and sometimes leaving them behind; she still bought good clothes, and liked to dress the twins smartly. She was lucky, Arthur said, not to have any rent to pay.

As well as being fond of the house, she was now rooted in Epping. She had made a good many friends, but they were not people whom Arthur and Mabel knew. Whole tracts of the countryside, which had been farmland when the Lamberts first came to Epping, were now covered with new houses, bought mainly by men with staff jobs in expanding industries – plastics and electronics – or by sales reps covering the north-eastern suburbs. Lorna seemed to gravitate toward these people, perhaps because they had taken over the Conservative Association from the retired colonels and landowners. It was also, naturally, a matter of age. Lorna played tennis and went to dances, so she met people who were of her own generation, including quite a few who were younger than she was.

These young people were always on the telephone, dropped in to see Lorna without notice, and invited themselves – or were invited by Lorna, usually when Mabel hadn't much food in the house – to meals. They all smoked and drank a great deal. They gave parties from which Lorna returned at two or three in the morning, roaring her car and banging doors. Lorna also gave parties, or gathered so many friends for an evening that it amounted to a party. While Arthur and Mabel took refuge in the front room, or went to bed and tried to sleep, the guests talked in loud voices, put on pop records – probably maltreating Arthur's hi-fi – and rolled up the carpet to dance. In the morning, Lorna was apologetic. But it happened again and again.

One night – it was a beautiful summer night, with a full moon – Arthur and Mabel were woken by shouts and laughter from the garden. Lorna's laugh, which had become shriller with time, was clearly distinguishable. Her friends were swimming. One man chased a girl round the lawn and, despite her screams, threw her into the pool with a resounding splash. Amazed, Mabel saw that the swimmers were stark naked.

'Disgusting!' Arthur said.

'Oh dear,' said Mabel, 'I do hope the boys haven't woken up.'

'This is too much. I'm going to call the police.'

'Arthur – you can't!'

He didn't, but when Lorna said in the morning: 'I'm afraid things got a bit out of hand,' he replied grimly: 'They certainly did.' Mabel tried to make allowances. They must have come without swimming costumes, young people had to enjoy themselves, and – as Arthur himself often said – times had changed. She was always making allowances nowadays, not only for Lorna's friends but for Lorna herself. Lorna was a sweet girl at heart, and she'd been through such a bad time. Still, the bad time was quite a long while ago, and Mabel couldn't conceal from herself that Lorna had changed. She was inconsiderate, she no longer helped much in the house, she was short-tempered with the children and nowadays with Mabel too. Mabel tried to convince herself that she was still fond of Lorna, for she didn't want to think of what life would be like if she ceased to be so. A few serious words, she decided at regular intervals, would make all the difference. But she never spoke the words. She had always detested scenes, and she was afraid of anything like a row with Lorna. She wondered sometimes if she was afraid of Lorna; it was an appalling thought.

Arthur too, partly from nature and partly from pessimism as to the outcome, avoided conflict with Lorna. But his attitude to her had changed drastically. 'We judged our son wrongly,' he told Mabel. 'We didn't know what he had to put up with.' Jim had been right, in particular, about Lorna's extravagance. 'She's the same as ever, isn't she, only now it's at out expense.' She didn't need a car when she could (within reason) borrow Arthur's, she didn't need all those fancy clothes, and what she spent on cigarettes and liquor was disgraceful.

Most of the spending, to be accurate, was still at Jim's expense. However, Lorna wasn't above a few dodges, such as asking Mabel to get cigarettes while she was at the supermarket and forgetting to pay her back. In any case, having three extra people in the house wasn't something that Arthur had reckoned on at his age. Heating all the rooms cost money, having the lights on half the night cost money, laundry cost money, and Lorna and the twins were all healthy eaters. At the outset, neither Arthur nor Mabel had thought of asking Lorna to contribute to the household expenses. It was difficult to raise the question years later, but Arthur felt strongly that she ought to have offered.

Arthur now claimed that Lorna had only been asked to stay for a short time, and said flatly that he wished she would clear out. But, on top of the unpleasantness of telling her so, she simply couldn't go unless she had more money.

'She could find a job,' Arthur said. 'She can still type, I suppose.'

'Oh, that's just like a man!' Mabel protested. 'Working, and running a home all alone, and looking after the boys – I'd like to see you do it.'

The other possibility was that Lorna might get married again. Arthur said that this was what he'd been hoping for all along. Five years after the divorce – it took about five years for Arthur's changed attitude to crystallize – the expectation still seemed reasonable. She was heavier round the waist and hips and her face was losing its perfection of outline, but she was by any standard a desirable woman. She could be charming when she cared to. A man could well fall in love with her and be blind to her faults – like Jim, as Arthur acidly remarked. And she came across plenty of eligible men, some single, some divorced.

However, she didn't seem to be interested in men. When she went out, she drove off alone and returned alone; she was always with a crowd, not with anyone in particular. So far as could be seen, she was steering clear of any involvement that could lead to marriage, and indeed of sex. There was plenty of loose behaviour in her set, punctuated by occasional scandals, but although Arthur was ready by now to believe the worst of Lorna, the evidence indicated that she had no affairs.

So Arthur and Mabel had no choice but to put up with what they'd landed themselves with. And Mabel, though she no longer got any pleasure from Lorna's presence in the house, would have hated to see David and Jonathan go. They were getting quieter as they grew older – Lorna's discipline was effective – and they were very fond of their Granny. Mabel could forget all her troubles when she settled down with them in the playroom to work on a nice big jigsaw puzzle.

Arthur was coming up for retirement age. He had always planned to sell the house and move to a bungalow on the south coast, or else a cottage in some peaceful village. Property values in Epping were rising fast, so the profit on the exchange would have been a handsome addition to his modest pension. There was no sense anyway in staying on in the big house, for rates were rising too. But with Lorna in occupation, the whole idea was impossible.

When he retired, things were worse than he'd expected. He had reached a point at which the mere sight of Lorna was an irritant to him. If he settled down in the lounge, she would drift in with a couple of friends; they would drink gin and tonic and talk their nonsense, ignoring him after an offhand greeting. If he tried to do some quiet gardening, she would establish herself nearby with her transistor radio playing pop music. His only refuge was the front room, and even from there he could hear her endless phone conversations and her maddening laugh. He couldn't imagine how Mabel had stood it all these years.

Conflict was inevitable, despite Arthur's principle of avoiding it. He was getting more cantankerous with the years, and his resentment was always simmering. 'That was a nice table until you started putting glasses on it,' he would say, or: 'Would it be too much to have a short period of silence while I read the paper?' Lorna sometimes tried to mollify him, but often she snapped back. If there were no real rows, it was only because he retreated to grumble to Mabel.

One day, when she invaded the lounge with a friend – a woman he particularly disliked, divorced and said to be the tart of the new district – he stalked out and went for a walk. It was raining, so his departure was clearly demonstrative. When he came back, the friend had gone. Lorna was lounging on the couch, smoking a cigarette. (Ash on the carpet again. Though Mabel put ashtrays everywhere, she never managed to be near one.)

'Sorry about that,' she said.

'I've got used to it,' Arthur replied.

She sighed, implying that she wasn't to blame for his intolerance.

'Look, Father, we've got to stop getting in each other's hair. It hasn't been easy for either of us since you've been at home all the time, has it? I want to make a suggestion. Wouldn't it be better all round if I had my part of the house and you and Mother had yours?'

Arthur pondered. 'I suppose it would,' he said.

He remembered the old days when Jim and Lorna had stayed for a couple of months at a time. They'd lived upstairs, using the playroom when they wanted to be alone. Downstairs – the lounge especially – had belonged to Arthur and Mabel. It had worked well.

But that wasn't what Lorna had in mind.

'We could make the playroom into a nice sitting-room for you. The boys are over the play stage, really. I wouldn't have to bother you at all. You wouldn't even notice when I had friends in here. And the boys could use the front room to do their homework.'

Arthur stared at her. He couldn't find words for his reaction to this outrageous demand. He mumbled something about thinking it over, and marched off to the kitchen to explode to Mabel: 'You'll never guess what Lorna's had the nerve to suggest!'

Yet, on consideration, there was a case for agreeing. Three people with a busy social life – the boys had started to bring friends home – did need more space than an old couple. If Arthur and Mabel had the lounge, Lorna's parties would be held in the playroom and sleep would be impossible. She wouldn't accept that counter-proposal, anyway; the choice was between continuing the present situation and giving her what she wanted. Any form of separation, Arthur decided in the end, was better than none.

Besides, there was a financial advantage. He could put in separate meters and make Lorna responsible for heat and light in the downstairs rooms. With a shrug, Lorna agreed to this.

So the change was made. Arthur moved his books, his hi-fi and the two old comfortable armchairs up to his new sitting-room. Lorna bought two modern chairs, aluminium with black plastic seats; the lounge did look less cluttered. Arthur and Mabel didn't have to see her at all except at meals, and not always that, since she was given to snacks at odd times.

All the same, Arthur didn't enjoy his retirement. Probably he wouldn't have enjoyed it in any event; he had been fond of his work and he hadn't many resources. A man can't read and listen to music all day and every day. He took to going for long walks in Epping Forest, in almost any weather. Mabel didn't go with him. She had never been able to match his stride on her short legs, and now she was plagued by arthritis, so it was as much as she could do to walk to the shops and back.

One autumn afternoon, two years after his retirement, Arthur didn't come home from his walk. When it got dark, Mabel phoned the police. They found him in a remote clearing. Death had been due to a stroke, the doctor said.

Jim and Lorna met at the funeral, for the first time since the divorce. They shook hands and exchanged a few sentences. But when Mabel asked Jim if he would come back to the house, he said: 'I don't think I will if you don't mind, Mum.'

In the evening, when Mabel stared at Arthur's empty chair, she felt desperately alone. Lorna had gone out somewhere; the twins came upstairs and asked if they could do anything, but she knew they had homework. She would have liked to die at the same time as Arthur – and like Arthur, quickly, without an illness. But she was only sixty-four. She might have many more years to get through.

It was lonely being a widow, she found. Some of her friends in Epping had moved away when the men retired, or were in poor health, or had died; those that remained seldom invited her or came to see her. She hadn't kept in close touch with her brothers and sisters, nor with Arthur's. Jim and Maggie came to London once a year, stayed at a hotel, and gave her a couple of meals, but she could see that they were fulfilling a duty. Lorna had her own life. The twins were still fond of their Granny, she tried to believe. But even this was doubtful; they were growing up fast. David was mad keen on cricket and football, while Jonathan – the clever one – read science books and fiddled with a chemistry set whenever he had a spare hour. Mabel had nothing to say that could interest them, nothing to offer them.

Then Lorna decided to send them to boarding-schools – public schools. Jonathan won a scholarship and Jim agreed to pay David's fees, although he and Maggie sent their own children to state schools. The twins seemed glad to go. They would be at different schools, so they wouldn't have to wear D and J on their clothes any more. And they weren't, to tell the truth, really fond of their mother.

Mabel spent a lot of time in a chair by the window, knitting or crocheting, and often just gazing down at the garden. Lorna had found a man to mow the lawn, but the herbaceous border and the rose-beds were a mess. It was Arthur who had done the gardening. Mabel couldn't manage it with her arthritis, and Lorna didn't care. Mabel didn't often go down to the garden, even in summer. It was awkward walking through the lounge – Lorna's lounge.

Except for the kitchen, which the two women were obliged to share, there was now a strict demarcation of territory. Lorna complained if Mabel left her umbrella or her shopping-bag in the front hall. She complained frequently, even when Mabel had tried to be helpful. If Mabel took a phone message while Lorna was out, it was: 'Didn't he say where I could reach him? Didn't you ask? You might try to think, Mother.' If Mabel did the washing-up, which Lorna neglected for days, it was: 'Where the hell have you put the glasses? You know I don't use that cupboard.'

Mabel never answered back. She accepted that Lorna would never again show her any kindness or affection; that Lorna had changed completely, or had come out in her true colours – it didn't matter which. Without Arthur to make a stand, she was utterly submissive to Lorna, and very much afraid of her. This fear had even a physical aspect. With her spine bent and her shoulders bowed, Mabel felt that she had shrunk. Lorna had put on a lot of weight, but because of her height she didn't look fat so much as big – hefty like the Soviet athletes you saw on television, menacingly powerful.

Lorna now did most of the shopping, since Mabel found it increasingly difficult to get about, but she regularly faced Mabel with demands for money. 'You must chip in on the food, Mother – I've had to get new tyres for the car, and new garden chairs, I really can't manage everything.' Mabel had the impression that she did more than chip in, but didn't dare to argue. However, she worried. Prices kept rising, and she had only the pension and Arthur's savings. She was paying the rates, paying for repairs to the house, paying for the man to mow the lawn.

Four years after Arthur died, Mabel had a bad bout of 'flu.

'It's nothing serious,' the doctor said, 'but you do need to stay in bed. Is there anyone to look after you?'

'Not really,' Mabel answered.

The doctor frowned. He was new to the district, but he had probably heard something about Lorna.

'I think I'm going to pop you into hospital,' he said. 'Just to see that you get a real rest and a bit of cosseting.'

When Mabel came home – really feeling much better for the rest and the friendly smiles of the young nurses – Lorna said to her: 'I think we ought to do something about the house, Mother.'

'How do you mean?'

'It's still in your name, isn't it?'

'Yes.'

'I'd be happier if it were in my name. It's only a formality, of course. But if anything happened to you it would go to Jim, and I don't fancy living here by Jim's permission.'

Mabel felt that there were dangers for her in this change, but she didn't object. Curiously, she found herself being sorry for Lorna: a woman who had never, since childhood, had a home in which she was completely secure, in which she didn't live (at least in legal theory) by someone's permission.

Anyway, in reality the house was already Lorna's more than it was Mabel's, and had been ever since Arthur's death, or indeed since she and Arthur had surrendered the main rooms.

'Will you pay the rates?' she ventured to ask.

'Oh yes,' Lorna said, as though yielding to an unreasonable demand to gratify a silly old woman. 'I'll have to pay the rates somehow, I quite see that.'

So now the house was Lorna's in every sense. And yet, not entirely Lorna's. She developed a habit of looking into Mabel's rooms on various pretexts and remarking: 'You ought to get rid of that old wardrobe, you know' or 'This room needs a complete painting job, honestly.' It was as though she couldn't rest until every corner of the house was under her absolute control.

Sometimes, Mabel tried to remember the lovely girl whom Jim had brought home years ago. But it was not easy. Lorna's beauty had collapsed, in the way that blondes of her type must beware of in their forties. She had a double chin, sagging lips, piggy eyes set in puffy flesh.

When Jonathan was sixteen, he suddenly announced that he didn't want to live with his mother and grandmother any more. He had formed, or renewed, an attachment to his father. Apparently he got on well with Maggie and her children, and they would be pleased to give him a home, at least during the school holidays.

Lorna said calmly: 'Well, you're old enough to know your own mind. If that's your decision, that's your decision.'

Mabel waited for her to add that she hoped to see him from time to time. Jonathan was evidently waiting for the same thing. They waited in vain; the boy stood up abruptly and went to pack his belongings.

The house was still home for David, but he wasn't there very often. He now had a passion for outdoor sports, the more adventurous the better. Every holiday, he was off on an Outward Bound course, or skiing, or mountain-climbing, or sailing. Lorna let him do as he pleased, merely grumbling when she had to sign cheques.

At the age of eighteen, David was killed climbing in North Wales. Apparently one of the party had been lost in a sudden mist; David had gone to look for him, and had missed a foothold and fallen down a cliff-face. It was two days before his body was found.

Through the anxious waiting, Mabel was in tears most of the time. She had always, with a faint sense of guilt, loved David a little more than his clever brother. Lorna was calm – brave, Mabel would have said years ago. But now, Mabel knew better.

A police inspector came to the house with the final terrible news. Lorna covered her eyes with her hand. The gesture looked rehearsed, as in a bad actress.

When the inspector had gone, she said: 'Well, that's that, I suppose.'

Mabel began to cry again, not for David but for Lorna. She had never loved her husband, never loved her sons, never loved anyone in her life. You had to feel sorry for her – what else was there to feel?

But Mabel didn't cry for herself, even when her arthritis was so bad that it was an agony to climb into bed. She was over seventy; she had lived her life. She had endured sorrows, disappointments, humiliations. But she had known what it was to be happy. Sitting by her window, she counted over her memories like a treasure that would not waste.

When Lorna told her that she must go into a Council home for old people, she made no protest. She didn't want to go; she would have liked to die where she had lived, among her own things and Arthur's things. But there was no sense in arguing, so she hoped that it wouldn't be too bad. Jim would come and see her occasionally, and perhaps Jonathan.

Lorna drove her to the home and saw her through the formalities.

'Goodbye then, Mother. I'm sure you'll be well looked after. Let me know if you've forgotten anything.'

'No, I'm sure I've got all I'll need, dear. Don't you wait, now.'

'All right.'

Lorna drove home fast, waving cheerfully when she saw a friend, but not stopping. When she reached the house, she stood and gazed at it for a minute. Then she turned her key firmly in the door.

EZRA

You must know the name, if you have ever bought dress material or curtains. In textile design, 'Ezra' leads the field. Awards have been so numerous that they no longer matter, all the magazines have done feature articles, and discerning department-store buyers from Stockholm to Sao Paulo place regular orders.

Yet there is something rather mysterious about 'Ezra'. It has no London office. It is to be found, the articles tell you, in a plain greystone house high up on a lonely stretch of the Lancashire moors. Visitors are discouraged; you notice, as you read, that the house has been photographed from a distance. You also notice that there are no interviews with the designers. The head of the team is known to be a woman called Joan Postgate. This Joan Postgate – Miss Postgate – answers letters, signs contracts, and is chairman of the company (a private company, of course). Few people, even in the trade, have actually met her or any of the other designers. If there are others – some say that she does it all herself.

Why 'Ezra', anyway? What can be the connection between textile design and an Old Testament prophet? One theory is that it's an acronym: that the original team – fifty or more years ago – consisted of four people whose names began with E, Z, R and A. But that's only a guess, and as a matter of fact a wrong guess.

The answers must be there, in the house. The address doesn't tell you much: Moor Farm, Radburn, Lancashire. Radburn is the village huddled in the valley, two miles away and five hundred feet down from the house.

Sometimes a magazine writer, exceptionally conscientious, tries to talk to people in Radburn. He never gets anywhere. As well as the professional mystery, there seem to be other mysteries of another order – personal, to do with Miss Postgate and the house on the moors. Strange things might turn up, it's hinted, if they were looked into. What sort of things? No one knows for sure, or no one will tell.

One person in Radburn could tell – Lily Holmes. But Lily is a frightened girl, and she doesn't talk.

If there were an investigation. . . . It has been considered more than once; there is a file in police archives. Lily has been interviewed. But Chief Constables have, in the end, decided to take no action. Why explode a scandal, bringing down the reporters and the television cameras, in a quiet and contented part of the country? Why wreck the lives of people who, presumably, are happy in their own fashion? Above all, why destroy a successful business that brings prestige and export earnings to Britain?

One fact is perfectly straightforward: the origin of the name 'Ezra'. It was simply the name of the man who made the designs in the earlier period, Ezra Postgate. (In some north-country families, these Biblical names are traditional.) When he began to make a hit with manufacturers, and needed a trade-name, his wife said: 'Why not Ezra?' The mystery arose only because, in what was then the custom, he always signed himself E. T. Postgate.

There is also a sound reason why the Postgates settled in such a lonely house. Mrs Postgate – Ruth – was consumptive. At that time, tuberculosis was often inexorably fatal; Ruth knew that, at best, she could only gain some years by living in healthy surroundings. The clean upland air and fresh winds of Moor Farm seemed ideal, or at all events the best choice for people who couldn't afford Switzerland. It had failed as a farm, like many marginal hill farms, so the house – though it was a big house and, in its austere way, beautiful – was going cheap.

Nobody in Radburn knew much about the Postgates. Coming from Yorkshire, they were regarded in Lancashire as strangers. Nor did anyone, as time passed, get to know them well. But if they chose to keep themselves to themselves, and evidently felt no need of friendships, this was considered to be their own business. Besides, they had good reasons not to go to the village more often than necessary. Ruth needed plenty of rest and couldn't walk far, especially up a steep hill (they didn't have a car). As for Ezra, he worked very hard. Late at night, the light in his workshop was like a beacon in the darkness of the moors. Occasionally, he was seen to catch the early morning train to Manchester with a portfolio of his work, returning by the last train in the evening.

Had anyone asked about them, he would have been told – it was a fact that leaped to mind – that they were a handsome couple. Or even, in Radburn's most lavish phrase, a lovely couple. They were both tall, slender and fair-haired (actually, the Scandinavian type found here and there in Yorkshire) with the kind of firm and graceful beauty that draws a willing admiration. Their rare good looks, and their contentment with each other's company, indicated that they were deeply in love. Ruth's illness was felt by everyone in Radburn to be a tragedy.

They were . . . one can't say popular, in view of their self-imposed isolation, but well thought of. Their talent was respected; it was known that Ruth worked with her husband, as much as her health allowed, and some of the successful designs were hers. Nor were they thought to be peculiar people, engaged in an incomprehensible activity, as 'artists' might have been considered in a place like Radburn. Their work was obviously useful, it had a market value, it served the cotton industry which was Lancashire's mainstay and was going through hard times.

The Postgates had one child, born a couple of years after they came to Moor Farm. The village people were surprised and, to some extent, disapproving. Ezra at least must be aware that Ruth couldn't live until the child was grown; the creation of a new life seemed merely to give added poignancy to her predictable fate. The general view was that 'it must have just happened'. But the truth was that Ezra and Ruth had taken a conscious decision after earnest thought. He very much wanted to be a father. He had a deep feeling, too, that his gifts – or rather his gifts and Ruth's gifts – ought to be perpetuated. For her part, Ruth didn't want to die without the experience of motherhood. That happiness, she believed, would relieve the distress that lay ahead.

What about the child? He (or she) would be scarred by Ruth's death; that had to be reckoned with. But he (or she) would begin life surrounded by love and devotion, far more so than the average child – particularly as he (or she) was sure to be beautiful and talented. And after Ruth died, this love would continue. It was Ruth who looked to this future, which Ezra preferred not to think about. Perhaps he would marry again, she thought, although he declared that he never would. Otherwise, she could trust him to be both father and mother; he really was very fond of children.

The child was a girl, named Joan. She was indeed beautiful, with the corn-yellow hair of the Postgates; her mother didn't have it bobbed in the prevailing fashion, but let it grow in long tresses. Her father cared for her, played with her, and took her for walks, carrying her on his shoulders over the moors. This cut into his working time, but life was becoming easier for him. Making head-way against the ebb-tide of the depression, he was beginning to establish the reputation of 'Ezra'.

Joan went to the village school. Her talent for drawing – accurate, well-proportioned drawing – was outstanding, but she was slow at learning to read and didn't seem particularly intelligent. The teacher, with a large class covering several ages, allowed each child to follow his or her bent, provided that the child kept quiet and behaved well, as Joan always did. She was, in fact, a very quiet girl. During break, instead of joining in games in the playground, she chose to stay in the classroom and work at her drawing; and as soon as school was over she set off to walk home. She didn't make friends. Apparently, like her parents, she didn't need any.

Ruth's last decline was harrowing, more harrowing than Ezra had expected. She had been calm and resigned over the years since she had known her illness, but toward the end she succumbed to panic. She became fervently religious (she had always been a believer, whereas Ezra was not); she prayed desperately, forcing out the words between coughs, and was tormented by the idea that she was going to hell. Often, she clasped Joan to her breast and sobbed. Much against his will, but seeing no option, Ezra sent the child away to a boarding-school. Soon afterwards, Ruth died. Joan was eight.

The effect of this loss on Ezra was also not what he had expected. He grieved, certainly. But he began to feel, almost at once, an impulse to reach out for happiness. Not happiness, exactly – that was out of the question – but distraction, fun, gaiety, everything of which he had willingly deprived himself while Ruth lived. His earnings were considerable, now that the depression had eased up. It was the year before the war, whose clear approach caused a hectic grabbing at pleasure. Joan, so far as he could tell from her letters, was contented at school. So long as he was abreast of his work, there was nothing to keep him in the lonely house. He made longish visits to London, and once to Paris. Girls were attracted to him; he was under forty and still strikingly handsome. He liked to play tennis with them in summer, to skate with them in winter, and to dance with them at any time. It was a demand for physical activity and excitement, another recompense for deprivation. But if a girl wanted him to meet her friends, to go dancing or skating in a group, his essentially reserved nature made him resist.

With one of these girls, Sally, he began a real affair. He picked her up at the Chelsea Arts Ball in the early hours of the New Year, 1939. She was an art student, still unsure of her direction; painting gave her pleasure, but she didn't believe that she had a distinctive talent. Ezra suggested that she should go in for textile design. She was grateful for the advice and for his casual but inspired tuition. As for the affair, it was intermittent – depending on his trips to London – and light-hearted, but quite passionate and, for both of them, highly enjoyable. Sally was a bright, cheerful girl, always fun to be with.

The war began. Sally's art school, a small private one, shut down. She sat at home, at a loose end and bored; she didn't get on with her parents. Ezra spent a weekend with her at a hotel, but with wartime travel difficulties they saw that it would be difficult to do this often. So he asked her to live with him, in the dual capacity of mistress and assistant.

She hesitated. The charm of the affair had derived partly from its now-and-then quality, and she wasn't sure that it would work at continuous close quarters. Besides, she wasn't a country girl and she qualied at the thought of a lonely house on the moors. On the other hand, London was no fun now and would be dangerous if bombing started. Also, she didn't want to be forced into uniform or a factory; she had come to think of textile design as a possible career, and working with Ezra was obviously a first-rate opportunity. In any case, while she didn't think of herself as in love, she was genuinely fond of him. So she made up her mind, and came to Moor Farm.

For a time, she was perfectly contented with her new life. You missed parties and theatres if you were kept at home in London by 'flu, she reflected, but you didn't miss them if they belonged to another world. Ezra's independence gave her an independence of her own, and she didn't even care to meet local people or go down to the village pubs. The work was fascinating; she was proud when he assured her that she made a real contribution. Relaxing by the fire, or gazing out of the window at silent starry nights, she felt as happy as she'd ever been.

In the village, Sally's arrival caused diverse reactions. People who adhered to a strict moral code were stern in condemnation. The more tolerant argued that a man needed a woman; the fact that Sally wasn't given the status of a wife indicated respect for the memory of Ruth. But in any case, Mr Postgate wasn't the kind of man who cared what other people thought.

When Sally found that she was pregnant, she was a little afraid to tell Ezra. The affair was still only an affair, and this complication struck a jarring note. But he wasn't at all put out. Indeed, the expression in his eyes told her – much to her surprise – that he was delighted. Male pride, she thought.

'I'll marry you,' he said at once.

'I'm not asking you to do that,' she replied. 'I mean, I don't think it's a good reason for getting married.'

'It's for you to say, my dear.'

'You don't actually want to marry me, do you?'

He fiddled with a pencil. 'Not really.'

'Then you shouldn't.'

'I'm thinking of the child.'

'There doesn't have to be a child. I'll go to London. Some of my friends know the ropes.'

But Ezra wouldn't hear of an abortion. It was murder, he said – it was evil. Sally, knowing that he didn't subscribe to orthodox morality or religion, was astonished by the solemnity with which he declared these principles.

'I've got to go through with it, not you,' she pointed out.

'I know that. But the child exists; it's my child as well as yours. And I don't choose to destroy my child.'

66

So she resigned herself, saying with a grin: 'Oh well, it won't be the only little bastard to come out of this war.'

In fact, it wasn't in Sally's nature to take things tragically, nor to look far ahead. What sort of life the kid could look forward to, she didn't quite see. She wasn't committed, even now, to spending her life with Ezra. But, whether they stayed together or not, he would concern himself with the child's future and put up any necessary money. He took full responsibility – reached out for it, indeed – and obviously he was very fond of children.

The child was a boy, and was named Michael. Sally shouldered the task of motherhood good-humouredly, but didn't mind admitting that she preferred designing fabrics to washing nappies. Ezra shared the chores willingly. He had got used to it, he said, when Joan was a baby and Ruth wasn't allowed to tire herself. 'Willingly' was an understatement – he really seemed to enjoy giving the child his bath and lulling him to sleep.

His feelings for his son were unmistakably strong and deep. Sally saw that Michael held a central place in Ezra's life, while she did not. But she hadn't imagined, all along, that Ezra loved her as he had loved Ruth. That is, as she guessed that he had loved Ruth; he was reluctant to talk about his wife to his mistress.

Now and again – over fairly trivial matters – they had sharp words. Sally found this natural; they were prolonging, through force of circumstances, what had started out as a casual intimacy. She was surprised that each of these incidents caused him real distress.

'Didn't you ever have a bit of a spat with Ruth?' she asked.

'No,' he said gravely. 'Never.'

'Oh, come on. All couples quarrel sometimes.'

'Well, we didn't.'

'Then all I can say is, there must have been something very special between you.'

'I suppose there was,' he said, and changed the subject.

Joan was with them during the school holidays. She was neither hostile to Sally nor at all fond of her; it didn't much matter to her, she implied, whether Sally was there or not. However, she was delighted to have a little brother. Clearly – and naturally, for a motherless child – she was very close to her father. Clearly too, he loved her as deeply as he loved Michael. He counted the days to the end of term, and was gloomy when she had to return to school.

Then he suddenly announced that he was taking Joan away from school. There had been an incident, in which he considered that she'd been unfairly punished; he took it very hard.

'I wish I'd never sent her away,' he said. 'It's much better for her to grow up at home.'

'That village school is pretty crumby, though, isn't it?' Sally remarked.

'I'll teach her myself. It's quite all right, if she reaches the normal standard.'

Officially it was not all right, since Ezra had neither a university degree nor a teaching diploma. And, Sally noticed, he devoted himself mainly to encouraging Joan's drawing; in other subjects his tuition was distinctly sketchy. But it was wartime, thousands of children were missing a proper education, and there were not enough inspectors to enforce the rules.

After another year, Ezra and Sally split up. Passion had faded, and love had never been a reality. The quarrels became more frequent and somewhat more serious. Perhaps they were exacerbated by Joan's presence; she behaved faultlessly, but Sally had a growing sense of being the least important person in the house. Anyway, by this time she was missing town life, variety, and friendships with people of her own age. She would have given up before now, she knew, if it hadn't been for Michael.

She put her cards on the table rationally. 'Let's face it, Ezra, this thing never was for keeps. We'd better pack it in before we really start making each other unhappy.'

He, too, was perfectly calm. 'If that's how you feel, I shouldn't attempt to keep you against your will.'

'We'll keep in touch,' she said. 'Of course, you'll be able to see Michael whenever you like.'

'Oh, Michael will stay here.'

She stared. 'What d'you mean?'

'Of course. This is his home.'

'You want me to give up my child?'

'You're the one who's leaving. I don't intend to give him up. And where would you take him? To live in some bed-sitting-room?'

Sally saw that he was absolutely determined – far more so than she was. She was fond of Michael, naturally, but when she examined her feelings she realized that she could live without him. Mothers normally kept children, to be sure; however, perhaps that was because the fathers didn't want them. It was undeniable that Ezra loved the boy more than she did, and that he could provide a better home. Sally didn't know where she was going – quite likely, to a bed-sitting-room. She would have to find a job. In any case, she wanted to live in a town, and children had to be in the country during the war.

So she kissed Michael, kissed Ezra, and left. Some months later, she fell really in love with a Navy lieutenant, in civilian life a promising young actor, and married him. She didn't consider it necessary to tell him that she had a child.

'Always looked like a flighty bit, that lass,' they said in Radburn. 'The little lad'll be best off with his Dad.'

One evening, at a crowded restaurant in Manchester, Ezra shared a table with a girl who ordered nothing but a cup of tea. Or rather, she didn't order it; the waitress simply brought it. The girl stared vacantly across the room. Her face was pretty at first glance, but shallow and uninteresting.

'I'm sure you're hungry,' Ezra said.

She rested her eyes on him vaguely and said: 'I'll eat later.'

'Eat now. I'm eating. What'll you have?'

'Sausages and chips, then.'

But she wasn't unwilling to talk. She had worked in this restaurant until she'd been dismissed. 'You can guess why,' she said. He could – she was visibly pregnant. She couldn't return to her parents in Wigan, she couldn't pay rent, so she was living with her friend, the waitress who took Ezra's order. When the place closed, the two girls would walk to the little room they shared. They shared a bed, too. It couldn't go on much longer.

Ezra said: 'I've plenty of room in my house. You can stay until . . . as long as it's necessary. Help in the house as much as you're able, that's all.'

She thought this over; her mind evidently worked slowly.

'Where is it?'

'Does that matter?'

'No, it doesn't really, does it?'

The girl – Linda – wasn't much help in the house, nor was she much of a companion. She sat in the kitchen most of the time, consuming as much tea as the ration allowed and listening to the radio. But Ezra and Joan had managed perfectly well since Sally's departure, and continued to do so.

The baby's father was an American soldier – Linda wasn't sure which one, among several possibilities. She was mildly grateful to Ezra for helping her and making no moral judgements. Of course, she thought, he couldn't preach. She soon grasped that he hadn't been married to Michael's mother.

Linda's baby was a girl. A fine girl, Ezra said; Linda, secretly, found the little creature rather repulsive.

'What are you going to call her?' Ezra asked.

'I don't know. P'raps you could think of something.'

He suggested Fay, and she agreed.

Ezra's reputation now stood pretty low, even among people who had been tolerant about his living with Sally. Sally had represented a kind of middle-class London bohemianism, which they hesitated to condemn just because it was alien. She had helped Ezra with his work, too; they'd had something in common. But Linda was just a common trollop, a Lancashire trollop of the kind that Radburn from time to time produced and cast out. It wasn't what they had expected of Mr Postgate. He had been keeping her in Manchester, they assumed; he needn't have installed her in his home, baby or no baby.

Linda, who went down to the village more than Sally had, sensed the feeling against her. She would have liked to explain that Fay wasn't Ezra's child; there was nothing between Ezra and her. But she couldn't explain things to people who already condemned her, and anyway this raised the question of whose child Fay was. Ezra was a strange man, she thought – a good man, but strange. After she got her figure back, she fully expected him to come to her room at night, but he didn't. (The explanation that she didn't attract him was naturally unwelcome to her.) What was she doing here, then? She was bored and restless – lonely, even unhappy although she knew she'd been lucky. She got no pleasure out of caring for her baby – less than Ezra, who behaved as though he were a proud father. She didn't like Joan or Michael, and she had no interest in Ezra's work.

'I can't stick around here for ever,' she told Ezra.

He looked up, giving her half his attention or less, from examining Joan's sketch-book.

'Oh? What d'you want to do?'

'Well, I ought to find a job.'

He guessed that she wanted to return to the life she'd been used to: pubs, all-night cafés, soldiers. This was true. But it was also true that she wanted a job; she'd worked, mostly as a waitress, ever since she'd left school. She liked to be told what to do and kept busy, instead of relying on her meagre resources to fill her time. She liked noise, jokes and back-chat, people coming and going.

'They'd have me back where I worked before, I reckon,' she said. 'Or somewhere like that, down in Manchester.'

'Well, you'd better go and look round.'

Her dull, pretty-at-first-glance face brightened. Then she said: 'About the kid.' (She seldom referred to Fay by name.)

'We can look after her, you know that.'

'Course, I'll come for her when I get settled.'

'All right.'

As Ezra expected, Linda never reappeared. He was fond of little Fay already, as he always got fond of children, and perfectly ready to bring her up as his own. It was an unofficial, doubtless an illegal, adoption, but no officials bothered him. Joan knew about how Ezra had come across Linda; Michael knew, and Fay herself knew, when they were older. No one else did. When the younger children went to the village school, they were known as Michael Postgate and Fay Postgate. As usual, Ezra didn't care what people thought.

It was after the war that the 'Ezra' designs became not merely commercially successful, but fashionable and then famous. Britain had to earn, to export, and do it in new ways. There was a new respect for the original and the creative: for British films, the Covent Garden ballet, modern architecture, and visual design of the 'Ezra' kind. This was the time of the first awards, exhibitions and feature articles. The mood percolated to Radburn; people grasped that they could be proud of the clever man at Moor Farm. There was no longer any point in levelling moral reproaches. The trollop had gone, all the children were well brought up and nicely behaved, and Mr Postgate's personal life was now impeccable. Indeed, the more fame and money he gained, the more rarely did he leave home. Of course, he was getting older.

People also took a favourable view of Joan, or Miss Postgate as she gradually came to be called. The beautiful child hadn't turned into a beautiful young woman. She was good-looking enough – would find a husband all right, no doubt – but that was all. Under the abundant hair, now brown rather than golden, her face was broad and strong – a face with character. She had a healthy, sturdy figure, without the slender grace that might have been her inheritance. This appearance suited her personality. Joan was capable, hard-working, and a great help to her father. She ran the house efficiently (despite the money, there was still no domestic help); she was a real mother to the little ones; and, in her late teens, she was a serious textile designer.

It was true, indeed – although no one outside the house knew exactly what Ezra did and what Joan did – that the business could not have flourished so splendidly without her. After years of training, she had become extremely skilful and reliable, with an infallible sense of the market and of what would catch on. She lacked her father's originality, his capacity for exciting new departures; but she could improve and develop every idea that she mastered, leaving him time to imagine and experiment. Besides, she took over the books and the correspondence.

Then, to the general astonishment, Ezra had his last adventure and added another child to the family.

He was in London, in 1950, to meet a group of American buyers. He was a virtual recluse by now, and had yielded only to urgent pleading by textile manufacturers and Board of Trade officials; the Americans insisted on seeing the creator of 'Ezra'. There was a party at their hotel, to which Ezra had to be dragged. He stood in a corner and talked to a girl who said with an engaging smile that she didn't know anybody and the whole thing was a ghastly bind. She worked for an agency, and had been hired by one of the Americans as a temporary secretary.

Her name was Carla; her family was Italian, though she'd always lived in London. She was very dark – her hair a lustrous black, her skin almost brown enough to be an Indian's – and small, with the delicate perfection of a figurine. Because Ezra had never in his life been attracted by this type of girl, she was irresistible to him.

She, on the other hand, had a weakness for well-preserved men of over fifty. Ezra's mane of white hair and sinewy hands were absolutely in her line.

They slipped away from the party and went to her flat. Ezra had intended to go home next day; he stayed for a week. Carla told her employer she was ill, and told her lover that she didn't want to go out. Once, he persuaded her to go dancing. Otherwise, they ate, drank and made love. He was a in a daze of irresponsible joy, reverting – long after he had ceased to expect it – to the mood of eager pleasure-seeking that had seized him after Ruth's death.

When he finally went home, Joan was furious. She was fully an adult by now, and it was no use trying to hide what he'd been doing – not that this would have occurred to him.

'Who is she, then?'

'A secretary. A girl who lives on her own.'

'Are you going to see her again?'

'I may. I haven't decided.'

'What do you need her for – a girl like that? This is where you belong.'

He worked, and tried to put Carla out of his mind. The serious, concentrated faces bent over their drawing-boards – Joan's, and nowadays young Michael's – rebuked him. But he couldn't resign himself to regarding the affair as over, although he had to admit that Carla probably did. He wrote to her, and got no answer. After about three months, availing himself of the kind of invitation that he normally ignored, he went to London again.

When he rang her bell, Carla opened the door and looked at him coolly.

'Oh, it's you.'

'I had to come. You didn't answer my letters.'

'No, I didn't. Well, you'd better come in.'

She had a work-table in her flat which he hadn't seen before.

'Yes, I'm planning to work at home. Typing manuscripts.' She smiled at him, ironically rather than affectionately. 'Keep me going while I'm having my baby.'

'Why didn't you tell me, Carla?'

'What for? It's my problem.'

'Not just yours. You're carrying my child, aren't you?'

'Oh yes, it's yours all right, don't worry about that. We really went wild, didn't we?'

73

'And d'you think I'm not concerned?'

'Look, lover-man' – she had disliked the name Ezra – 'we had a fantastic week, but it's over. I've got my life, you've got yours. This little postscript doesn't make any difference.'

He realized that he had wondered all along whether she might be pregnant; that was why he hadn't been able to forget the affair. He had wondered – and, deep down, he had hoped. Now, his fear was that she would destroy the child. But, she said, she wasn't considering that. The idea was repugnant to her, as much as to him. Besides, she was a Catholic. She made up her own list of sins and absolved herself for fornication, but took a grave view of abortion.

She was willing to accept a cheque, and promised to write to him from time to time, but she said that she didn't want to see him again.

The letters were infrequent, and merely reassured him that she was keeping well. He asked what hospital she would be going into, but she didn't say. Ezra distrusted hospitals – Ruth had died at home, all the children had been born at home. He kept worrying lest something should go wrong; Carla was so small, she had narrow hips. When he reckoned that the baby was nearly due, he went to London again.

This time, when he rang the bell, she looked out of the window and threw down the key. She was in a dressing-gown.

'D'you want to see your son? There he is.'

'Good heavens, I didn't know.'

'I was going to write. I've been a bit pulled down. He came early, about a month early actually. Tiny little thing he is – not going to be a bit like you. But he's quite OK.'

Ezra gazed at the baby, who had a puckered little face topped by dense black hair, and prowled round the flat. There was a smell of formula-food.

'Aren't you feeding him, Carla?'

'What, tit-wise? No, it's such a bind. The doctor said not to, anyway. Don't create an attachment.'

'Don't what?'

'Well, he's going to be adopted, obviously.'

'Indeed?'

'Yes, indeed. I've made all the arrangements. What else can I do? I've got my life to live.'

Ezra collected up the feeding-bottle, the formula, and all the

other baby-things, and started to pack them in a carrier-bag.
'What the hell are you doing?'
'If you're not willing to care for him, I am.'
'You're crazy.'
Ezra gently picked up the baby, who was fast asleep.
'This can't be real! You'll get into trouble. The adoption's all
fixed up, I tell you. You're absolutely insane.'
He shook her off as he went down the stairs. Outside, he picked
up a taxi. He went to his hotel, ordered a car and chauffeur, and set
off for Radburn.

Some time passed before the village people realized that there was
a new baby at Moor Farm. Some suggested that it could be Joan's,
but this was easily disproved. Mr Postgate had been gadding about
again, evidently. On the whole, there was more amused admiration
than criticism. Pretty good going, at his age! (Though he wasn't old,
when you thought of it, not much above fifty, and strong as a
horse.) And you couldn't say that he left the girls to carry the can.
Always was fond of children, of course.

When the little boy started to go to the village school, he was
called Mark Postgate.

Michael was taking the bus every day to go to grammar school.
There, he was liked and admired – more by the teachers than by
other boys, however. In the Postgate fashion, he chose to get along
without friendships. He was fair-haired and decidedly good-looking
– clearly his father's son. He had sailed through the eleven-plus, and
even in the testing atmosphere of a good grammar school he was
equal to all demands. The headmaster discerned what brings joy to
every such headmaster's heart: first-class intelligence, a true high-
flyer, university potential. It was merely a question of whether to
point him toward the humanities or the sciences, for he excelled in
both. Also, he had inherited an artistic talent that was already
remarkable. This, the headmaster feared, was a fatal gift. Young
Postgate could get anywhere, given a free choice; but it was all too
likely that a future as a textile designer was an ordained destiny.

Michael's talent was of the kind that needs only a pencil and the
back of an envelope to create, with dazzling swiftness, something
wholly individual and authentically imaginative. He was impatient
of detail; he hadn't Joan's capacity for discipline and precision. What
he had was a creative power of the same nature as Ezra's.

Fay was at the secondary modern; she'd been as certain to fail the eleven-plus as Michael to pass it. Like her mother, she was quite simply rather dim. Nor had she a trace of artistic talent, as Ezra was obliged to admit after earnest attempts to coach her. It wasn't, he reminded himself, in the blood.

But she was lovely. Strangely – or perhaps not strangely, if one knew who her father was – she was first a beautiful child and then a beautiful girl. It was an appealing, fragile beauty: pale skin, limpid blue eyes, hair of an even lighter shade than Postgate hair. The fragility was real, for Fay was not at all strong; she was away from school with bad bouts of 'flu every winter, another reason why she stood no chance in exams. The teachers treated her gently. She was sweet-natured, she responded gratefully to any encouragement, she did her best even when she was lost and baffled. She would be happy in life, surely, if her health stood up.

Meanwhile. Joan wasn't married. As time passed, she seemed reconciled to a spinster's life. In Radburn, she never met anyone on social terms (this was her own choice, to be sure). But – since her father never went anywhere nowadays, and since she managed the business side of 'Ezra' – she went to Manchester, to the various cotton towns, occasionally to London. Men invited her to dinner or the theatre. She accepted; she kept up a conversation and behaved in a civil, even a friendly manner. However, she rebuffed any advances, whether of a casually sexual or a more serious kind. 'I'm sorry, I'm not interested,' she would say firmly. The man was made to feel that he'd blundered, misunderstood her somehow. Perhaps she had an attachment nearer home, perhaps she'd been wounded by some unfortunate experience, perhaps she was a Lesbian . . . the man wasn't to know, and was never attracted strongly enough to wonder for long.

If she needed company, she had her father and her brother Michael. She was almost always with one or the other, or with both: working, discussing ideas for new designs, or taking long walks in the hill country. Ezra didn't care for outings, other than walks; but Joan and Michael sometimes drove a considerable distance to have dinner, and returned late. Isolated pubs with beautiful views were gradually being converted into good restaurants, patronized by businessmen who preferred to get away from their home towns. The Postgates now had a big, powerful car, their sole luxury. Joan was an excellent driver.

They could talk for hours, Joan and Michael. At this time of his life, he read insatiably and was constantly full of new knowledge and new ideas. Joan, with her truncated education, easily forgot that he was years younger. She loved to listen to him, her eyes held by his animated face and his expressive gestures. These evenings were far more stimulating than evenings out in London. Coming home on summer nights, she felt that she hadn't had enough, pulled off the road and stopped the car. No one disturbed them; other cars were parked at discreet intervals.

This was her only escape from a constantly busy life. She managed the business, she managed the house, she looked after little Mark, she nursed Fay through her illnesses. It would have been quite awkward if Joan had wanted to get married, unless perhaps to a man who would come to live at Moor Farm. And she recoiled from that. The house had always been a closed, self-sufficient Postgate house. Sally and Linda had made brief irruptions, but that was long ago and they hadn't stayed. There had never been a man from the outside world, not even for a meal or a night.

Michael reached the sixth form. The headmaster begged to be allowed to enter him for Oxford, or any other university that Mr Postgate favoured. Alternatively, he could go to one of the best art colleges – the experience would be valuable even if he was committed to being a textile designer. But Ezra distrusted colleges as much as he distrusted schools, hospitals, government departments and all other institutions. Indeed, he distrusted art colleges in particular. Michael was quite ready to start work as an equal member of the 'Ezra' team, he decided. And Michael fully agreed. He was content with his home; he had no desire to live in lodgings, in a town. Above all, he'd had enough of being taught. He was eager to create.

Fay left school at the same time. There was really no point in her staying on past the age of fifteen. Up on the moors, probably she wouldn't catch so many colds.

It would have been hard to maintain that these decisions were wrong. As soon as Michael got the opportunity, he produced brilliant work, just what was needed now that his father's inventiveness was somewhat declining. 'Ezra' took on a new lease of life; the awards and the export earnings came in thick and fast. As for Fay, she was both healthier and happier. She busied herself in the house, taking some of the load off Joan's shoulders. She was rather good at sewing and knitting, and grateful whenever she was praised. She even read some of Michael's books. Apparently she wasn't quite so dim as she had seemed; it was only in a school that she couldn't learn, as Ezra pointed out.

Joan had always been kind to Fay when she was a child, but now she treated her with a shade of condescension – rather, one might say, as a second-class citizen of the tiny republic. When Michael explained something to Fay, which he did with great patience, Joan was likely to interrupt and seize his attention. She didn't allow Fay to come when they went out to dinner, on the grounds that she wasn't old enough and would only be bored. (Michael had gone out at fifteen, of course.) Nor was Fay allowed to enter the workshop; Joan swept and tidied it herself. There was a bond between all the rest of them – the bond of creative ability. Little Mark's drawings were already promising. Joan set up a barrier, tacit but firm, against anyone who lacked this title to full rights. That is, against anyone who wasn't a real Postgate.

Fay, with her sweet and submissive nature, showed no signs of resenting Joan's attitude. She got all the affection she needed from Ezra and Michael. It was an odd kind of family by normal standards, but it was a happy home.

One day in 1960, Ezra said that he didn't feel well. This was so extraordinary that Joan asked: 'Shall I get the doctor?' The suggestion outraged him; he'd never seen a doctor in his life. He would lie down for a bit, that was all. An hour later, when Joan went to see how he was, he could neither move nor speak. She called the doctor. By the time he came, Ezra was dead.

It was hard to get over this loss. Ezra – with his inflexible will, his emphatic convictions, even his selfish and impulsive behaviour – had been truly the master of the house. Weeks and months later, the lack of his voice and his presence still seemed like a void in nature. Besides, Ezra had been in control of 'Ezra'. He hadn't done very much work in the last few years of his life; but Joan and Michael had relied on his experienced judgement, his approval or his veto. Now they had to get on without him.

Fortunately, there were plenty of designs in preparation and Michael was bursting with ideas. Manufacturers were used to dealing with Joan. The world at large, never having known that a man

78

named Ezra Postgate produced 'Ezra', saw no difference. So everything went ahead.

It was after Ezra's death that people in Radburn began to feel that Moor Farm was a strange place – to regard it with a mixture of bewilderment and suspicion. True, Ezra had been a strange man, they'd thought that for a long time; but individual oddity was to be reckoned with. It struck them now that there was something peculiar about everyone who lived in the house.

They hid themselves away, all of them – Joan and Michael and Fay. They held absolutely aloof from the village, and they had no friends or visitors from farther afield. One could understand a couple who kept themselves to themselves, like Ezra and Ruth years ago, or even a solitary man. For three young people, it was more puzzling.

Joan was thirty now; clearly, she'd given up thinking of marriage. Michael was twenty. When he turned twenty-one, there was no sign of any celebration. It was unnatural that he was never seen with a girl. After all, he was a fine-looking young man, the business was flourishing, there was money about. He went for a walk on the moors sometimes, but always with one or the other of his sisters. And how about Fay? She was seventeen when Ezra died, and lovely enough to have a choice of admirers. Sometimes one of the bolder Radburn youths followed her after she'd been in a shop and asked if she fancied going out one evening. She mumbled something inaudible and walked away.

Then there was the little one, Mark. He was strange too, although in a different way.

Unlike any of the other Postgate children, he did make friends at school. At nine years old, he was the leader of a gang. He was small for his age, and wouldn't have stood much chance in a playground fight, but he had a curious power to make other kids do as he told them.

Under a new headmaster, the Radburn primary school was going overboard for new educational methods, much distrusted by parents. Teachers didn't keep order as in the old days, or even teach. It was all projects, free expression, unstructured lessons. The snag was that a kid with devilment in him could take advantage – and Mark took full advantage. He was clever, no doubt of that, but he was idle. He was, again in contrast to the other Postgates, high-spirited and mischeivous. If a drama period was disrupted by deafening chanting of improper rhymes, if a bucket of tar was smuggled into school and set on fire, if mice were let loose – you could bet that Mark Postgate was at the bottom of it.

Not that you could ever pin it on him. He was cunning enough to know when the teachers would have their backs turned. He knew their weaknesses, too. Some (young women from sheltered homes) were helpless in the face of bad behaviour; some (idealists with modern notions) didn't believe in tracking down an offender or in collective punishment. Mark's strength was his sharp perception of adult character. He was like a spy, dodging about as though in enemy territory, on an endless sabotage mission. He even looked alien, with his dark complexion and his small, glinting black eyes – who on earth could his mother have been? Just to catch sight of him, with a secretive grin on his face, plotting unpredictable villainies, made people uneasy. Radburn wasn't used to this kind of child. Indeed, one couldn't altogether think of him as a child. He had a child's irresponsibility and wilfulness, but a shrewdness and self-reliance that were far from child-like.

Evidently, no one had any control over him. It wasn't clear who was the head of the family – Joan because she was the eldest, or Michael because he was a man. Quite often Mark missed school, even for days at a time, and simply stayed at home. The progressive headmaster was reluctant to invoke the truancy rules, and the teachers found Mark's absence a relief.

Michael had got into the habit of working at night, like his father long ago. Joan preferred the rule of early to bed and early to rise. But he said that he worked best alone, when the house was even quieter than during the day.

One night, about a year and a half after Ezra's death, Joan woke at two o'clock. She wasn't sure why; the wind was raging round the house, but she wasn't often disturbed by high winds, nor by dreams. She might have been dreaming, she thought. At least, she had an unusual sense of anxiety.

She decided to get up and make Michael a cup of tea. When she took it to the workshop, he wasn't there. His work looked as though it had been abruptly abandoned.

She was suddenly certain that he wasn't in his bedroom. She went there, knocked, then opened the door. The room was empty.

Joan hurried to Fay's room. Leaning against the door, she could hear two murmuring voices. She stood for a long time in the cold corridor, tense and rigid, hearing everything – hushed laughter, sighs, gasps of pleasure, the creak of the bed. She went away only when she heard Michael moving about the room, getting dressed.

The next day, Joan struggled to control herself in the face of the intolerable. Intolerable it was, if for no other reason, because of the deceit, the secrecy. How long had it been going on, how long had it been hidden from her? The house – her house, the Postgate house – held an intimate joy that belonged to two people alone. Fay shared in it; she, Joan, was excluded from it.

She packed Mark off to school, though he'd counted that day on staying at home. In the workshop, a yard from Michael, she worked clumsily and without her usual care. In the afternoon, she gave up – she couldn't remember ever doing that before – and sat in the living-room, pretending to read and staring grimly out at a garden sodden with rain. Fay was sewing; she watched Joan timidly, not daring to speak, then retreated to the kitchen.

When she had made supper, she darted up to the workshop. Michael turned to her, ready for her kiss. She said: 'You mustn't come tonight.'

'Why not?'

'She knows.'

'What, Joan? How can she? What makes you think that?'

'I'm sure she knows.'

For two more days, the three of them circled warily about one another. Joan watched Michael fiercely, intercepting every glance in Fay's direction. Michael watched Joan; he still doubted, because he didn't want to believe, that she knew. Fay effaced herself, keeping out of the way as much as possible, looking silently down at her plate during meals.

Then – defiantly, to see what would happen – Michael announced that he was going to work late. He settled down in the workshop and waited for Joan to go to bed. Eleven struck, then twelve. She was still in the living-room, reading so far as he knew.

At last, as he'd half expected, she came to the workshop. He faced her boldly.

'Aren't you going to bed, Joan?'

'I'm not sleepy. I'll stay with you.'

She sat down at her drawing-board. They worked side by side for a time, as they did during the day.

His patience gave out before hers. He said abruptly: 'You've got to leave me alone sometimes. I'm not a child.'

'You're a fool,' she said.

'What does that mean?'

'You're a fool, like Dad. A pretty face, and you're knocked endways.'

'It's not like that. Fay and I are in love.'

'In love!' Joan's voice was scornful. 'You don't know what love is. You just want easy pickings. At least Dad went to London to find what he needed.'

'We're in love,' Michael repeated. 'We know each other well enough to be sure, I should think.'

'You know each other all right. Did you imagine I'd never find out?'

'Well, now you have found out. I'm not ashamed, don't think that. I'm a man. And Fay's old enough to know her mind.'

'You'll carry on like this, then?'

'We shan't stop loving each other. I've promised her that, and she's promised me. I expect we'll get married.' He hadn't spoken of this to Fay, but suddenly he was determined on it.

'You'll never marry her,' Joan said in a hard voice.

'Who's to stop me?'

'I'll stop you. For your own sake. You'd be tired of her in a year. A silly little thing, not a brain in her head – can't even understand the work we're doing, let alone help with it! She's handy for you, that's all. Dropped here by a tart, and tart she is herself. Dad had his tarts too, but he didn't talk of being in love, nor marry them either.'

'Is that all?'

'That's all for now.'

'It's enough. If you speak of Fay like that again, or if you take your bad temper out on her, I'll never forgive you.'

'So you think now. You'll live to thank me. Goodnight, Michael.'

It was an impossible situation. But impossible situations can endure for a time, and this one endured for three months. Behind a façade of normal life and work, the atmosphere in the house was strained and nervous. It was a bad time, and it was made worse because Mark was there.

In the long spells of embarrassed silence, his dark eyes gleamed, keen and vigilant. He noted – at least, the others felt that he noted – every change of expression and every clue to suppressed emotion. He turned up in parts of the house where he wasn't expected to be, always with a plausible excuse. And he got up at night, claiming that he wanted to go to the lavatory or to get a glass of water. How much did he understand? Everything, perhaps – why not? He was ten years old, he had always lived among older people, he had never been like an ordinary child.

Joan slept badly. Woken by the slightest noise, she lay tense and alert in the darkness. During the day she couldn't relax, even when she had Michael under her eyes and Fay was elsewhere. But she was a strong woman, strong in both mind and body. So she was able to keep up a steady, deliberate pressure. She treated Fay with scrupulous politeness, even consideration – the consideration of a home-owner toward a guest. Fay was often excused household tasks, on the grounds that she looked tired or she wasn't well. But when the girl tried to do her usual housework, Joan calmly pointed out her inadequacies. She had forgotten this, she hadn't managed to finish that, she hadn't grasped what she'd been told. Meanwhile, Joan was always close to Michael and always stressing what they shared. She adjusted herself to his timetable, starting work late in the morning and continuing in the evening. They embarked on a new series of designs. She praised his ideas, suggested possible modifications, discussed them endlessly in the workshop or in front of Fay in the living-room.

Fay suffered. She was passionately in love with Michael; but passion bewildered her, and sometimes she longed for the lost placidity. She had been used to him as a sort of elder brother, immeasurably cleverer and more mature than she was – used to admiring him without claiming much of his attention. The unexpected intimacy with him was wonderful, but also daunting. Even before Joan found out about what they did at night, Fay hadn't been sure that it was right. It was immoral, obviously; if that didn't matter, as Michael said, then why did they conceal it? She was frightened by the demands of his virility, by the relentless pressure of his body and the furious grip of his hands, by the utter completeness of his possession of her and his penetration to her innermost being. And she was frightened by her own ecstasy, her wild and reckless abandonment, which tore her away from all her moorings. While he was no longer the Michael she'd known, she wasn't herself. He had changed her, mysteriously and irrevocably. For, while she trembled at the power of this new experience, she could no longer do without it. After she went to bed, she lay tossing and turning, impatient for him to come to her. On nights when he didn't come, she sobbed herself to sleep.

Joan's discovery and Joan's hostility were taken by Fay as a due punishment. She couldn't defy Joan; she felt herself already defeated. Joan was stronger, cleverer, more determined. And Michael – through his own strength and cleverness, his Postgate nature – belonged with Joan. She knew that he couldn't defend her when Joan criticized and humiliated her. She was weak, she was without skill or resources, she wasn't a combatant but the passive object of the struggle. It was true that she got tired and made a mess of her sewing and knitting. She went down with 'flu, as she had in childhood, and couldn't shake it off. She looked terrible, she thought – even to Michael, no doubt. Soon, he would cease to desire her. He still swore that he loved her, but after all she had nothing to attract him except her looks and her ready availability. He needed a woman, and soon he would find one – a gifted, self-confident woman, who would be a proper match for him and be judged worthy of him by Joan. If only she could stop loving him! She could never do that, but she searched miserably for a way of escape. Perhaps she could pretend not to love him and return to her old safe, submissive position in the house. But no, she wouldn't be able to endure the constant sight of him, the agony of longing for him. Perhaps she could somehow disappear. Perhaps she would die. That would be best, she thought.

It did cross Michael's mind, in fact, that he could break himself of this awkward passion. He rang up an old schoolmate, now a student at Leeds, and got himself invited for a weekend. As he expected, there was a party and a choice of girls. He kissed one, then another, but he didn't feel a spark of desire, so he got deliberately drunk and fell asleep. He wanted no one but Fay, he was unalterably in love with her – he was certain of it. So he must make Joan accept it. There was no other way.

At Moor Farm, he could scarcely get a few minutes alone with Fay without being interrupted by Joan, or else by Mark. Sometimes he went to her room, waiting until four or five in the morning, but the sense of being watched remained with them and they achieved nothing but a hasty, furtive physical release. Joan was due to go to London and he promised himself a rich night of freedom; however, she cancelled the trip and did the necessary business by phone. Then Fay went down with 'flu. Joan made her stay in bed and carried up her meals and her medicines; he didn't even see her.

He was made wretched by her misery, her pitiable defencelessness. But he was also sullenly angry. Joan's opposition was a check to his pride, to his demanding will. He loved Fay and he wanted her – damn it, he must have her! Why should he be deflected from his desire, why should he let anyone else shape the course of his life? It wasn't worth living, if one submitted to that. Yet he couldn't see, in the face of hard reality, what he was to do. He couldn't live for ever with Joan's forbidding enmity – after all, he worked with her every day – nor could he go on sneaking to Fay's room like a guilty schoolboy. Either way, Fay wouldn't stand the strain. And he feared, in his heart of hearts, that he couldn't stand it either. He was strong, but Joan was stronger. At least, she was more stubborn, more inflexible and patient. His kind of strength was suited to a battle, to staking everything on a head-on clash. In the long siege, Joan had the more determined character. He was afraid that he would break first.

He provoked the clash one afternoon in the workshop, without forethought and simply because his patience was wearing out.

'Look here, Joan,' he said, 'you've got to let me have Fay.'

She looked at him calmly.

'What d'you mean by have her? You know you can't marry her. I'm her guardian.'

This was news to him. Perhaps it was a bluff, he thought, but he was vague about things like this.

'Live with her, then.'

'Not so long as I'm here.'

'All right, we'll go away.'

'And what will you live on?'

She had him there. Though he was of full age, he still had no stake in the company. Joan and two Manchester businessmen were the directors. Michael had no money, except the savings account that he'd kept since boyhood. He had his skill as a designer, but jobs were not easy to find nowadays without formal training. Nevertheless, he said promptly: 'I'll get a job.'

'And live with Fay?'

'That's right.'

Joan left her work and stood close to him.

'You'll be in serious trouble.'

'Come off it. Lots of people live together without being married.'

'Brother and sister? Even half-sister – it's against the law.'

Michael stared at her.

'You know damn well Fay's mother was pregnant when Dad came across her. He just collected kids.'

'Try and get anyone to believe that.'

'You know it, Joan.'

'Do I?'

'Christ,' he said, 'you wouldn't do this to me, would you?'

She put both hands on his shoulders. Her eyes were fixed and dilated.

'I won't lose you, Michael. You never belonged anywhere but in this house.'

'I belong with Fay.'

'Do you think I'll let her take my man away from me?'

She kissed him, full on the lips.

He broke from her, wrenching himself from the strong grasp of her hands, and ran to his room. Later, she heard him leave the house. It was a cold winter day, but it would be like him to take a long walk on the moors.

Joan worked tranquilly on until it was time for supper. Michael hadn't come back, although it had long been dark. She wondered whether he'd spoken to Fay, and went to the kitchen. Fay had done nothing about making the meal. True, she wasn't completely over her 'flu.

It dawned on Joan that Fay wasn't in the house. Mark was able to enlighten her. Michael had gone out of the front door, and Fay ten minutes later out of the back. Mark had seen her cut across the old paddock, then join the road to the village.

'Why didn't you tell me, you brat?' Joan shouted.

'Mark gave her his sly smile. 'I don't mind if they go.'

Joan drove down to the station. They had taken the Manchester train.

Like most runaways, Michael and Fay went to London. They found a furnished room, and Michael thought of looking for work. As a freelance on commission, he wouldn't need an insurance card and could use a false name. But Fay was unhappy in London. The endless tangle of streets scared her, and she was sure that Joan would find them – Joan knew people in London. The room was expensive, everything was expensive, and Fay couldn't get her health back. They had better move on, Michael decided, while she was still fit to travel. They took the coach, saving the train fare, to Cornwall.

The sun shone; it was hardly like winter at all. Fay perked up, and they began to be happy. They found a room at a farm – full board for less than the room in London had cost. Fay, who had never seen the sea, loved walking along the cliffs. And they found work, using their false names. Michael was a gardener at a big house some miles away. Fay helped at busy times in the local pub.

But they were being watched – Fay was sure of it. Strange men, who didn't seem to belong to the neighbourhood, chatted her up in the pub and remarked on her accent. She was confused, unable to deny that she'd lived in Lancashire. Another strange man got off the bus when Michael travelled home from work, then went into a phone box.

They gave up working, and moved to another farm, at the end of a half-mile track from the road.

One day, as they were returning from a walk, they saw a car parked on the track. It was unmistakable – Joan's big car, now old and of a type no longer made. They dodged across fields. But they had been silhouetted against a clear sky on the brow of the cliff; they must have been seen.

They made love that night wildly, desperately.

Early in the morning, they walked up the cliff again. The sea, choppy in a west wind, beat on the rocks far below.

'I daren't jump,' Fay said. 'Push me.'

Michael clasped her in his arms. They fell together.

After the bodies were washed up, the coroner's court returned an open verdict. The Chief Constable was puzzled and, having established identity, consulted with his opposite number in Lancashire. It was decided not to pursue the case.

In Radburn, everyone was shocked. Such a fine lad – such a lovely girl! And what an awful death, being blown off a cliff by a gust of wind! They were a close family, those Postgates; it wasn't usual, a brother and sister going off on holiday. Some people muttered that the whole story hadn't been told. But there was nothing to go on, beyond uneasy speculation.

Joan resumed her life, plodding through a desert of stoical grief. Helpless, despairing grief was not in her nature. The loss of Michael was, like the loss of Ezra, precisely that: a loss. She regretted bitterly that she had been unable to hold him, but she didn't feel guilty. Men behaved unpredictably, she thought; they were weak, wayward, prone to foolish infatuations, blind to their own best interests. If anyone was to blame, it was Fay. The worthless little thing, unequal to making anything of her own life, had dragged Michael to death with her.

When Joan had to go to the village, she was calm and tight-lipped, accepting condolences with a dignity that repelled intrusive sympathy. She ceased to leave home, to visit Manchester or London. Business could be done adequately by letter or phone. The atmosphere of mystery which had always surrounded 'Ezra' deepened from this time onward; no one knew who produced the designs. In reality, Joan worked alone. She thought sometimes of recruiting designers to help her, but couldn't bring herself to do it. However, this was a difficult period. She knew her limitations; she was efficient and fully professional, but there was no one now to throw up the radically new, exciting ideas. For a time, she was sustained by the brilliant work that Michael had done in the year before his death. After that, 'Ezra' was somewhat in the doldrums. The business was solidly established and well respected, but no longer in the vanguard. Years passed without awards.

Joan was waiting for Mark to grow up and take his place in the Postgate tradition. He was gifted – there was no doubt of that. His drawings impressed her by their bold, vivid originality. But he was even more casual, more impatient of discipline and detail, than Michael had been at his age. And he wouldn't stick to his drawing-board for more than an hour; he liked to roam about on his bicycle, sometimes alone and sometimes with youngsters from the village. Joan was patient with him, cajoling him into the workshop, praising and encouraging, guiding him toward his destined future.

He had failed the eleven-plus, not through lack of brains but through idleness and indifference. He didn't mind going to the secondary modern, along with his gang. But, as Joan saw it, he was wasting his time there. She wanted to take him out of school – school had never done any of the Postgates much good. However, this wasn't so easy as it had been in the war. She found that she would have to engage tutors, and she didn't want strangers in the house. So Mark simply didn't go to school very much. Teachers and truancy officers wrote letters which were blandly ignored, or asked in vain for interviews with Miss Postgate. To avoid trouble, she invented illnesses for Mark, who was in fact thoroughly healthy. Measles, asthma, earache, toothache – anything that occurred to her, or that he suggested. The headmaster didn't believe her (the doctor was never called) but didn't dare to call her a liar.

By the time that Mark was fifteen and able to leave school, he willingly accepted – indeed, he had never questioned – that he would become a designer, an inheritor of 'Ezra'. His friends left school too and started work, some of them in towns down the valley, so he had nobody to knock about with. He became steadier, seeing the desirability of translating his talent into achievement. Soon he produced a design that was suitable for the market. This filled him with pride and with lasting enthusiasm. He still worked by fits and starts, sometimes idling away a day, but when he was in the right mood he was tireless and Joan had to persuade him to break off for meals.

And now, every year was a year of triumph for 'Ezra'. Manufacturers and buyers were delighted by a whole new range of designs. There seemed to be no end to the sheer creative richness that poured from the unknown team. Once again there were awards, public acclaim, the certainty of success.

It had never been easy to think of Mark as a child or a boy, and at eighteen he was fully a man. He was slightly built and a little below average height, but clearly this came from his mother's side and he was at his full stature. Yet, for a mixture of reasons – his unusual dark colouring, his boyhood reputation as a disturbing element, and the whole atmosphere of singularity, even mystery, which surrounded both Mark himself and the way of life from which he derived – people were uneasy with him, a little fearful when they saw him coming. His purposes and his thoughts were his own, not to be readily guessed, not in the ordinary run.

Girls were fascinated by him, however. He dressed elegantly and in the latest style; wherever he bought his clothes, it wasn't in the same shops as other Radburn young men. Long hair had come into fashion and gave him another advantage, for his hair caught the eye with its black gleam. When he wore an open shirt, the girls noticed that hair grew thick on his chest too.

A strange thing about Mark Postgate was that you never knew when or where you might see him next. He had a powerful motor-cycle which he rode very fast – some said recklessly, others said with a perfect calculation of how to skirt danger – and for long distances. Many people in Radburn had cars nowadays, and they told of being overtaken by Mark at astonishing speed, sometimes on the motorway, sometimes on winding mountain roads. He wasn't – he had never been – so consistently solitary as the other Postgates. From time to time he would go into a pub, buy drinks generously all round, and put away an impressive amount of whisky himself, though it didn't seem to affect him. Or he would come to a dance and dance with several girls – seldom with the same girl twice. But his appearance always caused surprise and gave the impression that he'd been seized by a sudden mood. Most of the time, he had no need of any company but his sister's; they were very close, in the Postgate way. So a week, a fortnight, three weeks could go by without his being seen at all. Apparently, he simply didn't go out of the house. But then again, for all that anyone knew, he might not be there. One didn't think of a Postgate doing anything so normal as going on holiday, but of course the money was there. Someone spoke of having caught a glimpse of him in a café in Spain. It might not have been Mark – a lot of Spaniards looked like Mark – but quite possibly it might.

People began to wonder, as they had wondered about Michael ten years ago, why Mark didn't have a girl. He was eighteen, then nineteen, then twenty . . . still no girl. But, as with so many other things, one couldn't be sure. It wouldn't be like a Postgate to choose a local girl. Perhaps Mark found his girls when he was far from home, like his father before him.

It didn't seem credible that he was shy, or a late starter. It wasn't credible, certainly, to the Radburn girls. When a girl admitted to herself, after a dance or after trying to hold his attention in the pub, that she had failed to attract him, she felt that it was because of his experience, not the lack of it. She would wonder against whom, to stand a chance, she'd have to match herself. Presumably against some sophisticated creature in a wider world – an older woman, perhaps a married woman.

But he wasn't seen with anyone, except his sister. They drove, now and again, to one of the restaurants where she had dined with Michael. Obviously, if Joan wasn't taken out by Mark, she wouldn't be taken out by anyone else. She had made it sufficiently clear by this time that she didn't wish to marry nor to have anything to do with men. It was a pity; she was a fine figure of a woman, scarcely looking her age at forty, the kind of woman with whom a successful man of business would be proud to have his name linked. But she knew her own mind, doubtless. And after all, it wasn't extraordinary for a woman to be content with an absorbing career.

There were reasons – or there might be reasons – why Mark eluded the local girls, but it was surprising that he wasn't tempted by Lily Holmes. Many people thought, and Lily herself thought, that she would have suited him down to the ground. She was extremely attractive, she was intelligent and a lively companion, and her best subject at school had been art. She now worked, very capably, as the doctor's secretary. Because of her family circumstances, Lily had acquired a habit of independence. Her mother was dead, her brothers had left home, and she kept house for her father, a sales representative who was away for long hours, sometimes overnight. It was said, inevitably, that Lily took young men up to her bedroom when she had the house to herself. However, she was far from being a tart. If anything, she was distinctly choosy, as several hopefuls had discovered.

Since she was used to being the sought and not the seeker, she had to swallow some pride when she set her sights on Mark. But she had no choice; she was in love with him. It must be love, she decided as she examined a feeling more intense and compelling than any she had known before. Besides, his detachment and the speculation about him – everything that made him different – presented her with a challenge.

She succeeded, with the luck that favours those who watch for opportunities, in being on the spot whenever his spasmodic social impulses brought him to Radburn. They became, whether he admitted it or not, friends. She would take up a conversation where it had been left at their last meeting, ignoring an interval of weeks, and keep it going – questioning him, inviting his opinions, drawing him into argument – so that he was inextricably involved with her and other people were excluded. In the pub, she would say: 'Let's sit over there, shall we?' and secure a small corner table.

One night, having ensured that he stayed till closing time, she met his 'Goodnight' with: 'Aren't you going to walk me home?'

Her house was on the fringe of the village, up a lane that went on to a farm. She stumbled on a stone and took his arm. But she didn't stop talking. She was bored in the village, she told him; people were stuck in old ruts, they didn't think of making anything of their lives. She regarded her job as a time-filler. But she wouldn't get married, as most girls did, for the mere sake of security.

They reached her gate.

'I like talking to you,' she said. 'I can't say what I really feel to most people. I like being with you, Mark.'

He said nothing, and let go of her arm. Perhaps he was wary of being watched, she thought; the light shone full from the large front window of the house.

'When shall I see you again?' she asked daringly.

'I don't know.'

'Not in Radburn, if you'd rather not. There's a good film next week down in Rochdale.'

She wasn't pleased about pressing herself on him like this, but she had to be frank about her desire for him. He would call for her, he said. It was summer and good weather, so a trip of several miles was something to look forward to.

They went on Mark's motor-bike. Lily was scared by the pace at which he took corners, by the roaring of the big machine as it sped downhill; scared, but also excited. 'That was fun,' she said resolutely when they arrived. The evening was a success. They both liked the film, and they had a good meal at a Chinese restaurant. He was more at his ease with her, as she'd hoped, away from people who knew them.

Lily's father had gone to bed when they got back to her house, and they stood at the gate in darkness.

'Will you come in?' she asked.

He hesitated, then said in a tone that was oddly indecisive for him: 'No . . . I don't think so, thanks.' She couldn't read his expression.

'I'll be seeing you, then. Thanks for a lovely evening.'

She moved close to him and offered her lips. He kissed her swiftly, almost violently.

She had deliberately refrained, this time, from asking when they were to meet again. She had drawn him as far as possible, for the present. But he had taken her out, so she could assume that he would take her out again.

However, she neither saw him nor heard from him for over a fortnight. So far as she knew, he didn't come to Radburn even to buy something at a shop. She had no means of telling whether he was shutting himself up in Moor Farm, or away.

Her impatience for him took the form of a perpetual restlessness. She hated having to stay in the doctor's surgery or in her home. Whenever she could, she went for long walks alone. Several times, lured by hope, she passed by the house where Mark lived his mysterious life. It stood well back from the road and she couldn't see into it. She never caught a glimpse of him, nor of his sister.

One day, leaving her work at six o'clock, she set off to walk to the crest of the hills. Her father was away, so she wasn't obliged to go home and cook a meal. Suddenly, she heard the noise of a motor-bike. She waited for it, ardent and breathless. It didn't occur to her that it could be anyone but Mark.

He stopped. He had to; she was standing in the middle of the narrow country road.

'How did you get here?' he asked.

'I walked.'

'Long walk.'

'Give me a ride home, then.'

He started off, with Lily on the pillion clutching his waist, and headed toward Radburn. But he turned off at a crossroad and rode up another spur of the hills. On he went – up and down, north, south, east, west. At his usual speed, and in deepening twilight, it was a risky ride. But she didn't allow herself to think of that, in the joy of being with him.

At last he took her home. She leaned forward, still holding him, and pressed her cheek against his.

'Come in, Mark. I'll make you some supper.'

'There'll be supper for me at home.'

'Come in, Mark, please.'

The moment he took off his crash-helmet, she secured him in a close, passionate embrace. The demand was hers, at first; but when she drew away from him, he didn't let her go. She felt desire taking hold of him, past calculation or reversal.

'Oh, my darling,' she said. 'I've waited for you.'

'I know.'

She laughed contentedly. 'D'you want that supper?'

'No.'

She guided him upstairs. He made love to her without prelimi-naries, with an intent, driving concentration. Later, she wondered if he had strained to become absorbed in her – to banish a doubt or another loyalty. But at the time, she was simply consumed in her delight and her triumph. And she felt his sureness, his knowledge of how to possess and satisfy a woman.

She was lying in a happy day-dream, relaxed beside him, when he got out of bed and began to dress.

'Won't you stay, darling? My father's away.'

'No, I must go.'

'Because of your sister?'

He frowned. 'She worries when I'm out on my bike,' he said.

'Ring up, then.'

'I can't argue about it,' he said sharply. 'You've had what you wanted, haven't you?'

'Well, so have you.'

He tried to smile. 'Yes, that's true.'

'It was lovely, wasn't it? But I want you to stay. Not just to do it again – I want to be with you, talk to you, sleep close beside you and wake up with you. Because I love you.'

He bent down and kissed her, almost in time to stop her last words. Then he went quickly out of the room and down the stairs. She heard the roar of the motor-bike.

Again, there were days and days of waiting – longing, disappoint-ment, bewilderment. Lily knew about men who lost interest in a girl once they'd notched her up as a conquest. She wouldn't believe that Mark was like that. He had made no promises to her, he had never said that he loved her, but she would not renounce the vision of a future with him.

He didn't want to be tied down, she supposed. But she'd made no suggestion of that; she'd been careful, at the outset, to let him know that she wasn't set on marriage. She only wanted to offer him her love.

Was he afraid, perhaps, of his sister's disapproval? Lily couldn't see why; there was no great gulf, socially, between the Postgates and her own family. Didn't the sister want him to have a girl at all? She was twenty years older, had brought him up like a mother; possibly she resented his growing out of boyhood. Lily was aware of the curious closeness of the Postgates. The house on the moors seemed to hold them, to detach them from ordinary friendships and affections. She didn't know much about Joan. A reserved, uncommunicative woman, everyone said; but rational enough, surely, running a house and a good business. Once, meeting Joan in a shop, she tried to start a conversation about prices. Joan wasn't very forthcoming, but she was polite. Of course, she wasn't forthcoming with anyone.

About a week after this, Lily saw Mark at last. She had gone home to lunch, as her father was unwell and staying in bed, and she was returning to work. Mark was on his bike, buying petrol at the garage on the edge of Radburn.

She ran to him.

'Hello, Mark.'

Uneasily, dropping his eyes after a glance, he said: 'Hello, Lily.'

'I've been missing you.'

'I'm sorry.'

He paid for the petrol, and the attendant went to get the change.

'Don't you want to see me again?' she asked.

'I can't, Lily. I was wrong . . . I had no right to do what I did.'

'But why?'

'There's no future in it.'

'I don't see why not. You must give me a reason.'

His dark eyes suddenly looked straight at her.

'We're not like other people. That's all.'

'Who's not?'

'We? Postgates.'

'I don't understand.'

The man brought the change and lingered inquisitively.

'Goodbye, Lily,' Mark said, and started up the engine. The noise beat brutally at her ears.

She didn't understand, didn't understand at all. She was fearful now, anxious as well as puzzled. But she was also goaded, and determined not to be put off with an explanation that was no explanation, curtailed by the irritating chance of being in a public place.

She had made up her mind to invade the stronghold of the mystery – to go up to Moor Farm. She reached this decision quickly, one September evening, emboldened by a couple of drinks in the pub. If Mark opened the door, she would insist on a real talk with him. If she was confronted with Joan, she would try to make a good impression and be asked in. She had a plausible excuse; she was a volunteer in an Oxfam fund drive.

There was a light in one ground-floor room – a reading-light, she thought – but no one answered the bell. She noticed that the garage door was open and the car wasn't there, although the bike was. Joan and Mark must have gone out. Probably they wouldn't be back until it was unreasonably late for an Oxfam canvasser to call. But now that she was here, she was held by the longing for a sight of Mark, as well as by sheer curiosity. She sat down on a bench in the garden.

About half past ten, the car swept the drive with its lights. It was going fast until it braked; Lily was sure that she hadn't been seen. She watched Joan and Mark walk from the garage to the house and go in. For a moment, she had an impulse to stop them. But they were talking to each other, and she was deterred by a strong sense of the forbidding Postgate apartness.

Still, she couldn't bring herself to go away. A light went on upstairs. The curtains weren't drawn; no one could be expected to observe an isolated house. However, although some time passed, she couldn't see anyone moving about the room.

She made herself admit that she was being silly. She wasn't likely to see any more of Mark; for all that she knew, his room was at the back. So she got up and started to walk toward the gate. But it was a dark night, and she trod on a garden rake which had been left lying about. The thing sprang up and fell back, clattering on the drive.

Lily stood stock still. Then, compelled by her own defencelessness, she looked round. Joan was standing at the window of the lighted room. Standing there, stark naked.

As Lily stared, Mark came up behind Joan. He was naked too. He put his arms round her protectively, and she pressed her body against his. Swiftly, he drew the curtains.

Lily ran, blindly and recklessly. Her shoes crunched the gravel, she rattled the gate open and slammed it shut, but she was desperate to escape. She went on running down the road, afraid of being seen in the village, yet longing for its safe familiarity. The two miles seemed unbelievably long.

Halfway down, there was an empty cottage of the old-fashioned kind, once the home of a labourer on Moor Farm. It was a convenient, secluded place for lovers. A young man and a girl were walking up the hill toward it; they knew Lily well.

'Lily! Whatever's the matter?'

She tried to answer, but couldn't. Tears, held in until now by shock, began to stream down her face.

'Have you seen a ghost, love?'

She struggled for control, and tried to pretend that nothing was wrong. They offered to walk back to the village with her. She refused, and with some misgivings they let her go. To their questions, she yielded only a shuddering silence.

Rumours and suspicions spread like a dense, ugly cloud between Radburn and Moor Farm. They stemmed from pity for Lily: she'd been sweet on Mark Postgate, he'd surely had his way with her, then she had found out something – something unspeakable – and she was a changed girl. She no longer danced or went to the pub, she shrank timorously from men. People recalled and gathered together a long record of strange facts – Ezra's defiance of accepted convention, the fate of Michael and Fay, the unnatural self-sufficiency of all the Postgates. And, proving that they had something to hide, Joan and Mark emerged from their seclusion more rarely than ever. Joan, when she did come to the village, was served by shopkeepers with icy courtesy – not that she seemed to notice. Girls who had sighed for Mark now swore that they wouldn't let him touch them. But he wasn't seen any more in the pub or at dances, nor even out on his motor-bike.

Rumours and suspicions . . . They were no longer spread only by idle gossips; they were the concern of ministers of religion, of the doctor for whom Lily worked, and of the police. The cloud grew weightier and darker. It seemed likely to burst at any time.

But nothing happened. Slowly, the village has regained its

customary grudging tolerance. Perhaps, people say now, it isn't right to believe the worst. What isn't known for certain – what can't be understood – is best left alone. They are strange folk, the Postgate brother and sister, but they harm no one so long as no one meddles with them.

Inquiring outsiders still sense a mystery. But the village people won't talk – or rather, will talk only about 'Ezra'. About the awards, the sales in foreign markets, the magazine articles which some people collect in scrapbooks. Radburn has never lost its pride in 'Ezra'. They are thankful, in the end, that no rash action or unseemly intrusion has robbed them of that pride.

After all, it's a very successful business.

SENIOR CITIZENS

When Edgar Blake said that he was going to retire, his wife was taken by surprise.

'Are you really?'

'Well, I shall be sixty-five this year.'

'Yes, I suppose so.'

No more was said, for the moment. During more than thirty years of marriage, Iris Blake had grown accustomed to announcements that could only be acknowledged: 'I'll be staying in town tonight' . . . 'I'll be in Scotland over the weekend' . . . 'I've got to go to South Africa for a few weeks.' She and Edgar had not discussed anything, in the proper sense of the word, for years – actually, since they had discussed the schooling and progress of the children, who were by now grown up. A Sunday at home, like this, was marked by long periods of silence which neither he nor she found unnatural. She was glad to have him there, of course; he was her husband. But she fully expected him to read the papers, do the crossword, and go through some business reports, secluding himself for that purpose in an upstairs room which had been made into a study when it ceased to be the children's playroom. This was what he did, as usual, while she cooked lunch. The main difference between a Sunday when he was at home and a Sunday when he was away was that Iris made a real lunch, instead of a salad for herself.

While cooking, she adjusted herself to the fact that Edgar would be sixty-five on the tenth of July. She always remembered his

99

birthday and gave him a present, generally a tie or cuff-links, and she was clearer about the date than about his age. It seemed to Iris that age was significant only at the extremes of life. Through a long middle period one was simply a person, neither young nor old. That period lasted, she would have said if asked, from about thirty-five to seventy. But no: for a man, retirement brought it to a close at sixty-five. She had known this, doubtless, as a general fact, but hadn't connected it with Edgar. Until today, he had never mentioned the approach of retirement. Perhaps it hadn't been real to him either until the turn of the year (it was now the end of January).

Iris herself never thought about being old, about ceasing to be an active, busy middle-period woman. True, she was ten years younger than Edgar – almost eleven years, for her birthday was in April. But she hadn't been worried by this gap at the time of their marriage, and she had been virtually unaware of it for a long time now. She didn't think of Edgar, any more than of herself, as old or even 'elderly'. He was in good health, as she was. He was overweight, but he always had been. Perhaps not always, perhaps since forty or forty-five . . . she couldn't remember exactly.

During lunch, she looked at him more closely and reflectively than she had for years and tried to prepare herself for a new picture of him: a member of the older generation, a retired man, a man of leisure. But she couldn't relate this picture to the man sitting opposite her, stuffing food into his mouth. Edgar always ate quickly, as though he couldn't spare the time.

'What will you do after you've retired?' she asked.

'Oh, I don't know,' he said. 'Just take it easy, I should think. Be a nice change.'

She saw that he had no answer to this question. Perhaps he had been evading it, perhaps it hadn't occurred to him – about that, she couldn't guess. She thought about it on and off while he was in London, at work.

It was a question that yielded only negatives. Edgar had no interest in the affairs of Dorking, the town where they lived, although the decision to live there had originally been his. He wasn't a handy-man; they always employed a builder to decorate the house or make improvements. He wasn't keen on gardening, like some of their neighbours. The Blakes' garden was all lawn, except for a shrub-border which was Iris's concern. He didn't play chess or bridge, he didn't read much, he wasn't musical.

The retirement wasn't mentioned again for several weeks. Edgar made a trip abroad. When he came back he was very busy – as usual, or even more than usual. It was a point of honour with him, she imagined, not to give an impression (either at the office or to her) of slacking off. She hoped that retirement, when the day came, wouldn't find him unprepared; she had a vague feeling that he ought to be making plans. But perhaps that wasn't possible, or indeed necessary. How did one plan for taking it easy? Anyway, it was Edgar's business, not hers.

Then, one day in April – it was her birthday, which must have reminded him that his own wasn't far off – he said: 'I think we should move when I retire.'

'Move?' she repeated. 'Why?'

'Well, I shan't need to live near London, shall I?'

They were having dinner in a London restaurant, as they usually did on birthdays and anniversaries unless he was away. Edgar didn't enjoy these occasions. He grumbled about the service, which was never fast enough for him, or about the background music, or about the noisy conversation at other tables. Between him and Iris there was little conversation; as she'd remarked to a friend, you could tell whether a man was dining with his wife or with someone else, according to whether they talked or not. Nevertheless, Iris enjoyed being in a good restaurant – the lively atmosphere, the interesting clothes worn by other women, the dishes that she wouldn't have known how to cook. It occurred to her this evening that, since Edgar came on from his office, there would be fewer of these dinners after he retired. Dining out in Dorking was not the same.

And, if he meant what he said, they wouldn't even be living in Dorking.

'Where do you want to live?' she asked.

'Somewhere in the country.'

'But we live in the country now.'

'The real country. Dorking's become just a suburb, hasn't it?'

Iris didn't think so. Although many of the husbands were commuters, she knew Dorking as a town with its independent life. Besides, there was real country in the North Downs if you explored the small roads and lanes – Edgar only knew the route from home to the station. However, she merely said: 'Where did you have in mind?'

'Devon or Cornwall, I was thinking. On the sea – surely you'd like to live by the sea.'

'I'll think about it,' she said. They dropped the subject, but he returned to it when they got home and were going to bed. The house was too large, he said, ridiculously large for the two of them. However, it would fetch a good price. And they would need the money – the difference between this selling price and the buying price of a cosy little place in the West Country – in order to live in any kind of comfort. After his retirement, even the Surrey rates and the heating of the big house would be a burden.

'But you'll have a good pension, won't you?' Iris asked.

'Well . . . not enormous.'

He looked at her suddenly, turning round from hanging up his suit, and said: 'They ought to have made me a director. But they didn't.' She had never heard him speak with such bitterness.

Then he told her, for the first time, that he hadn't reached the high position in his firm which had been his due. She had never, as a matter of fact, been quite clear about what his position was at any particular point. She had assumed, in the later phase of his career, that he had an important job. That seemed to follow from his heavy responsibilities, his frequent conferences, and the journeys abroad. But she gathered now, although she didn't understand the hierarchy and his statements were not very explicit, that the job wasn't so important as she had imagined. She had supposed that he went abroad as some sort of negotiator – he had referred, impressively, to 'projects' – but apparently the truth was that he went as a salesman. A senior and trusted salesman, no doubt, yet still a salesman.

Iris wasn't greatly disturbed by this discovery. It cast no doubt on the qualities – integrity, loyalty, hard work – that Edgar had shown all his life. If he had lacked some other quality, it wasn't his fault. If the lack of promotion was an injustice, as he hinted, that was still less his fault. Had he expressed disappointment at some earlier time, she would have been not only sympathetic but involved. They might have discussed whether he should switch to another firm. But there it was: he didn't tell her, they didn't discuss, she wasn't involved. There was no sense in distressing herself about it now, when he was about to retire.

What mattered was his decision that they were to move. She had looked at the retirement as Edgar's concern, perhaps Edgar's problem. It wouldn't affect her, she had believed, except that she would have Edgar at home. But the move meant that her whole life would be changed quite as much as his, if not more. She loved the house, for one thing. It was her home, in a way that it had never been his. The improvements – the picture window, the fitted carpets, the patio at the back – had been her ideas and her satisfactions, not his; she had merely asked him whether the money was available. Dorking was her home, too. She had friends there, close friends, whereas Edgar had none. She had built up a life in Dorking, of which he knew as little as she knew of his working life, and she had never dreamed of abandoning it.

Yet she saw no possibility of getting him to change his decision. She didn't think of herself as a subservient wife, dominated by her husband. She had never opposed him because there had been no necessity, no occasion; his life and hers had been distinct, neither merging nor clashing. But, just because of this, if she set herself against this decision it would appear as unnatural interference. It wasn't even easy to see how they could argue. He had a strong case, obviously – he saw this move to a picturesque home by the sea as proper and correct, he felt that he deserved it, and the financial considerations were hard facts. To change his mind, he would need to see something – the value and fullness of her Dorking life – which he had never grasped, and which indeed she had never tried to express to him.

At all events, the move was a firm reality for Edgar. He got estate agents' lists from his chosen region and studied them earnestly whenever he was at home. Every weekend, if he could manage it, he drove west to look at houses. Iris sometimes went with him and sometimes not. She disliked the long drives – Edgar drove aggressively, fuming whenever he couldn't overtake – and also the task of going round other people's houses. Either the owners were at home, and she felt like an intruder, or the houses were empty, which meant chilly, damp and forlorn.

Anyway, she said, surely they could wait for better weather? That spring, it was always raining in the west. And after he'd actually retired, they would be able to make the trips without hurrying. But he was intent on pressing on with the search as though it were part of his work. 'We want to get settled in before winter, don't we?' There wasn't too much time, he said, to find the house, get through the process of moving, and complete any redecoration or alteration that might be needed.

Meanwhile, the house at Dorking was put on the market. This seemed illogical to Iris, when they hadn't yet found anything to buy; but Edgar explained that it was better to stay in a hotel for a short time, if necessary, than to risk being stuck with two houses and borrow at the current appalling interest rates. The task of showing prospective purchasers round the house fell to Iris. She hated it, she simply hated it. In the bedrooms especially, she felt all her life – her marriage, the childhood of John and Sheila, her serene middle age – being exposed to a cold scrutiny. Some of the people were rude and callous, making unfavourable comparisons in her hearing to other houses they had inspected. But she almost preferred them to the polite ones, who said: 'It's really nice, isn't it? It must be a wrench to leave.'

Her friends got to know, of course. 'Oh dear, we shall miss you,' they said. Iris put on a bright smile and said that they would have to manage without her. They seemed to assume that her home was already disintegrating – for instance, they offered their own homes instead of hers when she was due to have a coffee morning. And indeed everything that she had taken for granted was beginning to break apart, to sink into a dimmer and narrower space.

One Sunday night, Edgar came home – having driven all the way from Falmouth in the rain – and announced that he was finished with the West Country. The houses were nothing but jerry-built bungalows, and the prices were shocking. It wasn't that he couldn't afford them, assuming that he got a decent price for the Dorking house, but he refused on principle to pay more for a place than it was worth. He had decided to find a house in East Anglia. He should have done that to begin with – a chap in the office had been telling him about it. There were scores of solidly built old farmhouses, going dirt cheap because the area wasn't fashionable. But that was the best thing about it: it was genuine country, not spattered with caravan sites (Cornwall had changed since he'd first known it) and overrun by tourists half the year. And you got more sunshine in East Anglia; after all, it was the dry side of England.

The next weekend, he reported that he had found the very place.

He was so certain of it that he'd made a deposit. The weekend after, he took Iris to see it.

It was in Norfolk, a county which was entirely strange to Iris (and in fact to Edgar). The landscape – a landscape of unenclosed spaces, rather as she imagined some huge country, America or Canada – gave her a feeling of being lost, of wandering about and getting nowhere. Although Edgar drove fast, as usual, the towns and villages seemed to be very far apart. The weather increased the sense of strangeness. It was dry all right, but not at all warm considering that it was now June. When they got out of the car, she shivered in a keen easterly wind. Nothing here offered her a welcome; on the contrary, she felt intangible warnings, intimations that Norfolk didn't want her.

The house consisted of two farmworkers' cottages, knocked into one. It was a real country kind of house, faced with knobbly flints, and could be classed as picturesque, she supposed. Yet it didn't welcome her. It was hard, somehow – unadorned, unloved. Virginia creeper or clematis would help, she thought, but would take time.

'Where are we?' she asked.

Edgar showed her the map. He hadn't been able to find a house 'on' or 'by' the sea; but the sea was there, eight miles away, and there was a splendid beach, he assured her. In the other direction, the village was two miles away – an outline of a village with hardly any shops, she remembered from flashing through it. They were twelve miles from the nearest town. The house, standing on what passed in Norfolk for high ground – a plateau rather than a hill, so imperceptibly had it risen – commanded an extensive view. But a view without landmarks or scale, a view of nothing in particular. And the house itself had, so to speak, no position. There was no reason why it should be where it was, instead of a mile or so away in any direction.

They went into the house. The rooms looked quite big, as empty rooms always do, but not big enough to take all the furniture from Dorking. The conversion had been a thorough job, so that very little needed to be done. However, for some reason the people who had made the conversion hadn't stayed, and the house had been on the market for two years. This accounted for the price, which certainly was temptingly low. Iris saw that Edgar had, to his mind, brought off a magnificent coup by discovering this house, foolishly overlooked by all the people who were paying through the nose for bungalows in overcrowded Cornwall.

'I'm not sure,' she said. 'I'd like to think about it.'

This was just what she wasn't allowed to do. There was an offer for the Dorking house. Iris knew that she ought to be glad to let it go to Mr Foster, and not only because he was willing to pay the full price set by Edgar without haggling. Mr Foster and his wife were nice people, they had 'fallen in love' with the house, and they had four children, so it would live again as a true family home. Secretly, Iris found the Fosters' enthusiasm hard to bear. Strangers had no right, she felt obscurely, to love the house as she had loved it. It was as though the house would soon forget her and transfer its affections to the Fosters, while she found no welcome in Norfolk. But she had to yield it to them, whatever she felt. They had just come home from Singapore and were living in a furnished flat. Mr Foster indicated politely that he would be glad to have vacant possession as soon as possible.

So Iris agreed to buying the house in Norfolk. She couldn't reduce herself to being homeless, living in a hotel. Nor could she face a further period of searching. Why not make the best of the Norfolk house, since Edgar was set on it? And really, what difference did it make to her – Norfolk or Cornwall or anywhere else? Best, she decided, to get the whole agonising business over with.

At the last moment, when Edgar was counting the days to his retirement, he was asked to stay on to the end of August. It was the staff holiday season, someone was ill, there was a sudden pressure of business; he would be compensated for the disturbance of his plans. But the contracts were signed and the Fosters were counting on moving in. Iris said that she would look after the move to Norfolk.

There was a great deal to be done. She commandeered the car and drove several times between the two houses, getting up at the crack of dawn to beat the London traffic. She measured the new house meticulously to decide what pieces of furniture she could keep and where to put them. At first she hated to get rid of anything, but then she nerved herself to make a brutal clean sweep and sold off every piece that wasn't absolutely needed. The new house turned out to be smaller than she'd thought, once she tried to find a place for the big wing-chair or the heavy sideboard, and she was afraid of making it look smaller still by cramming it. She had to get new carpets, too, for it was only reasonable to let the Fosters have the fitted carpets. Then, as the house had been empty so long, she had to get the water and electricity reconnected, arrange for calor-gas (there was no main gas supply, naturally) and plead with the local bureaucracy for a phone. All this she did in a concentrated mood of resolute energy, thinking of nothing but the problem she had to deal with at the moment. She was grateful for the responsi-bility, the tight timetable, and the sheer physical weariness that helped her to drop into sleep every night, leaving her no chance to consider what was happening to her. What she felt about that she had felt already, and would perhaps feel in the future, but not now.

They agreed not to celebrate Edgar's sixty-fifth birthday; the real landmark would be his retirement. On the birthday, the tenth of July, Iris was in Norfolk. The Fosters had taken over the Dorking house a few days earlier, the furniture had been moved and installed, and she was already living in the new house after a couple of nights in a bed-and-breakfast place recommended by the estate agent. Edgar would come down at weekends; it was much too far from London to commute, of course, so the firm was paying for him to stay at a London hotel.

She got up, made breakfast, and drove to the village in order to phone Edgar from the kiosk – the phone for the house was faithfully promised, but not yet a reality. He was in conference. She left her birthday greetings with his secretary. Then, on an impulse, she decided to walk back to the house . . . walk home, she mentally corrected herself. Perhaps the countryside would become real for her; it was only space and time when she passed through it in the car. She could collect the car in the afternoon. There was a bus – a poor service, but she had the timetable.

It was a very hot day. Summer, in this part of the world, seemed to be brief and intense. There was no shade on the road, and after a quarter of an hour Iris decided that she was behaving ridiculously, but she tramped on. The road ran absolutely straight, so that she had the feeling of being in some newly settled country – not even America or Canada, but perhaps Africa – where roads connected self-contained settlements at great distances. But of course that was absurd. Norfolk had a long history, an immense memory of life and death, like any other part of England. It was only that she hadn't begun to link herself to this history, to anything that had happened or was happening here. She didn't belong. She looked to right and left, across huge fields, as though she might find a point of contact.

The air was utterly still, without a touch of wind. She walked through an infinity of silence, in which the clack of her shoes sounded like a trivial, ineffective interruption. There was no one to see her or hear her, and anyone who did see her wouldn't know who she was. It was extraordinary to live, to have her home, in a place where her existence was unknown – meaningless. She had a curious feeling, not simply of being completely alone, but of having ceased to be herself, Iris Blake. She had to define herself, and to explain by what paths she had come here.

Iris Perrier. It was a long time since she had thought of herself by that name. She had begun again with her marriage – begun again consciously, though without any great effort, since this had seemed to her normal. She had broken, quite willingly and indeed hopefully, with Iris Perrier. Now she was making another break: not such a complete break, since she was still married to Edgar, but a real break all the same. That took her back. There was a connection, which she had yet to explore, between the girl called Iris Perrier and the woman walking down this straight heat-sodden road, Iris Blake.

As a girl she had been – though this wasn't the kind of phrase she habitually used – somewhat unsure of her identity. Or rather, she had a false identity, imposed by her surname. The Perriers were of French origin, and Iris was committed at school and elsewhere to persistent and mostly vain attempts to get people to pronounce it in the French way. She didn't feel at all French, however, and she wasn't even good at French, so this assertion merely gave her an unreal distinction, like possessing an old title in a country that has long been republican.

Her immediate family was so small as scarcely to be a family at all. She was an only child. Both her parents had drifted away from – or offended, Iris didn't know – their own parents and other relatives. Her father died when she was twelve. Her memories were of long quiet evenings, in which she did her homework and her mother, who taught history at a private school, prepared the next day's lessons. There were seldom any visitors.

Home was a small flat in an old-fashioned block – broad tiled corridors, slow clanking lifts with heavy gates – on the fringes of Hampstead and Kilburn. They were rather poor, Iris supposed, although money was a topic discreetly avoided. Mr Perrier had been a civil servant, probably in a far from exalted position. Mrs Perrier must have gone back to work after his death out of necessity, though she didn't say so.

What sort of a girl was Iris Perrier, as she climbed the ladder of her grammar school? None of the other girls, presumably, would have been able to remember her in later years. Not very brainy, not very pretty, not very popular – but not strikingly the reverse of any of these. She'd had no special friends. She had been shy, perhaps, but she hadn't at the time thought of this as a trait of her character, nor as a problem to be overcome. She simply hadn't expected to be noticed much.

Her future was not charted, except in general terms. Her mother assumed that she would get married (Iris herself wasn't confident of it) but said that it was a good thing to work for a while and acquire some qualifications, if only to fall back on 'if anything happened'. Iris wasn't drawn to any particular career, so she took the most obvious option, a secretarial course. She found a job with an architectural partnership. It wasn't so interesting as she had hoped – mostly to do with tenders and contracts – but she was glad to find that she could do it competently.

She continued to live at home. Some girls shared flats, but nobody asked Iris, and anyway she didn't want to leave her mother alone – unless she got married, of course. She still had no close friends. But the people she worked with took her along to lunch, drinks, an occasional film, so she didn't feel unhappy.

She had no great hopes of attracting men. She couldn't often think of the right things to say, and knew that she didn't make amusing company. When she looked in the mirror she found herself rather insignificant – meagre, almost skinny, with no bust or hips to speak of. Still, now and again a young man took her out. Paul Sinclair, eventually, took her back to his flat and made it clear that he wanted to go to bed with her. She didn't think of making any objection. Over the next three months or so she made love with

Paul regularly – mostly in the afternoon or early evening, to avoid explaining things to her mother. Then he told her that he was involved with another girl. Iris took this calmly; really, she wasn't much surprised. She didn't make love with anyone for the next six months, because she wasn't asked. However, there were three more men up to the time of her marriage.

Iris was aware that men found her easy. This didn't worry her; she enjoyed making love, she couldn't pretend not to enjoy it, and if her candid gratitude gave the man an extra satisfaction, he was welcome to it. What did worry her was something else. There was no real intimacy – except the intimacy of the body, which seemed to exist on its own – between her and any of the men, even Paul with whom she'd had (she supposed this would be the word) an affair. She couldn't talk to them about things that mattered to her: the cloudiness of her future, the weakness of her identity. She didn't... it seemed silly, but she didn't know them well enough for that. She still had no close friends.

So, when Edgar Blake asked her to marry him, she agreed as readily as she had agreed to go to bed with Paul.

He had no connection with anyone she knew. They met in a quite unpredictable and indeed curious way: they were both witnesses to a car accident near her home. Iris was walking, while Edgar was driving and had to brake hard to avoid being involved in the pile-up. They had to attend court and hang about – Edgar grumbled, making it clear that his time was valuable – waiting for the case to come on. They lunched together. As they left the court, he said – apparently on impulse, though she realized later that he must have mulled it over – 'I suppose you're not free to see a show or something on Saturday, are you?' Three weeks later, they were engaged.

Edgar was thirty-three. 'Quite a bit older than you, dear,' Mrs Perrier said dubiously. But it didn't seem important to Iris. If anything, it was all to the good, for two reasons. Materially, he was secure in his career; she wasn't marrying for money, but it would be nice not to have to count the pennies. And he was mature enough to be making a considered choice, since it was obvious that he could have married sooner. Iris didn't understand why Edgar had chosen her, but she was grateful, as she had always been grateful for good fortune.

In reality, he was marrying Iris because he had decided to be married. Ideas – new departures – didn't come readily to his mind, but when they did, he acted on them with determination and without delay. Iris saw this clearly down the perspective of the years, walking along the road in Norfolk. She couldn't have seen it at the time.

Edgar took it for granted that she would give up her job. Never having seen it as a vocation, she didn't mind. He also decided to buy a house (his firm would help with the mortgage) out of London. He had been living in a flat – rather a nice flat, Iris thought – but the concepts of marriage and house-ownership were linked in his mind. And you couldn't get a decent-sized house, with a garden and a view, close into town unless you were rolling in money.

Iris could have said, had she wanted to argue, that she hadn't enjoyed London to the full. Her young men had never taken her out very lavishly, so she had little experience of the London that meant theatres, good restaurants, late nights, taxis, West End shopping. But a new life must mean a new life. In any case, Dorking – that was where they found a house – wasn't far out.

Being a wife was different from being a single girl, as Iris considered that it ought to be. While Paul Sinclair and the others had treated her with jovial comradeship, Edgar's attitude was a combination of the masterly and the tender. The tenderness was rather deliberate, rather conscientious, but that made her appreciative. He made a point of being 'gentle' with her in bed; did he believe, she wondered, that he was her first man? Or did he choose to act on this assumption, to exclude a past in which he had played no part? Anyway, he never asked her about other men, and she sensed that she wasn't meant to ask about the other girls whom, presumably, he'd had. It was the first of many areas of reticence.

Another was Edgar's work. She knew that he was in an import-export business. When she asked what was imported and exported, he replied with a list of commodities, some whose names were completely strange to her and others which rang a bell but which she couldn't have defined. Pyrethrum, for instance – was it a metal or a plastic? She didn't want to display her ignorance: not because Edgar would have minded but, on the contrary, because he preferred her to be ignorant, and this she resented, though not at all acutely or rebelliously. The commodities were not the point anyway, he said; the firm might be dealing in quite different things in a couple of years' time. It was all rather nebulous, in that the firm didn't produce or even transport anything at all, but only 'dealt in' this or that. Edgar's work was to make arrangements . . . make decisions . . . decisions sounded better, she felt. He also said that one had to be actually involved in order to see how it worked – to understand it, in fact. And to be Edgar's wife was not, of course, to be involved.

He certainly worked hard. He often had to stay late at the office or attend some obligatory social function, so that he wasn't home until nearly bedtime. Often, too, he had to work on business papers at home. This indicated to Iris that he was already quite important in the firm and would become more important by dint of hard work. At weekends, he used to sit in an armchair, or in the garden in summer, doing nothing much: listening vaguely to the radio, reading the Sunday papers, seldom talking. Iris realized from the beginning that he wasn't a talkative man. His air of solid sturdiness increased her respect for him – respect, at that time, was what she felt more than anything else.

The move to Dorking ruled out any chance of her entering a larger family circle – not that the possibilities were ever great. Edgar's parents were old and immobile. His brothers and sisters appeared at the wedding and were seldom seen thereafter. Mrs Perrier came to stay occasionally, but not for long; she didn't, after all, mind living alone. She died unexpectedly and, so to speak, unobtrusively when Iris was thirty. Iris reflected afterwards that, though nothing had ever been said, her mother hadn't been delighted by her marriage. Perhaps she had hoped for something more romantic.

Well, Edgar and Iris were not romantic people. It was hard to say, after so many years, whether she had ever been in love with him. She didn't remember putting that question to herself at the time, and certainly didn't remember 'falling in love', a phrase that she still regarded sceptically. She would probably have said that she loved Edgar as a wife loves her husband, which wasn't the same as the feeling one might have for a lover (Edgar had never been her lover; Paul had, in a sense, but she hadn't been 'in love' with him either). She hadn't, at all events, married for love. She had married for stability, and to acquire a clear and durable identity, and for

happiness. Had she been happy? A matter of definition. It was fair
to say that she hadn't been unhappy.

Fortunately – Iris saw now how fortunate it had been, saving her
from all dangers of loneliness, doubt or discontent – they had
children. First a boy and then a girl. As a mother, she felt herself
becoming a different person. She even changed physically, putting
on flesh everywhere and losing her meagre, insignificant look. She
ate the things the children liked – bread and jam, cakes, crumpets,
chocolate biscuits. A time came when she had to cut down in order
to keep what she could justifiably call her figure. This amused and
pleased her.

After the first few years, Edgar was away more often. When he
had to spend the evening in town he stayed overnight, instead of
dashing to Victoria for a late train as he had when they were first
married. It was silly, Iris agreed, for him to come home simply to
sleep. Also, the firm began to send him abroad. She took this to
mean added responsibility. She was always glad to see him back,
naturally, but she didn't miss him badly.

The children filled her life. There were so many decisions to
make, forcing her to exercise judgement and exert authority, as she
had never needed to before. How late could they stay up? Were
they watching too much television? Was John old enough to have
a bicycle, considering the dangers on the roads? Could Sheila be
allowed to ramble on the Downs, where there were rumours of
lurking perverts? If she were forbidden, wouldn't this only lead to
anxiety and nightmares? It was up to Iris, the mother – Edgar had
full confidence in her. This increased her own confidence in herself
until, by degrees, it became automatic. Some of the problems
couldn't be discussed with him because they arose when he was away.
After a time, she asked his opinion only to ratify a decision already
clear in her own mind, or even forgot to inform him of it.

Edgar wanted the children to go to private schools – not so much
wanted as assumed that they would. Iris found out that the local
primary school was excellent and willingly patronized by middle-
class parents; the road to grammar school and university was well
trodden. After a short discussion, Edgar accepted this, merely
commenting that things had changed since his day and that it was
a saving not to pay fees. Reports of day trips to Boulogne and
school journeys to the Lake District (remarkably cheap, too) im-

pressed him favourably; kids didn't know how lucky they were nowadays, he said. He always noted open evenings and school plays in his diary, but seldom managed to go. The children, Iris noticed, didn't mind so long as she went. They didn't connect their world with the remote, mysterious world into which their father disappeared.

Christmas and the annual holiday were the appointed times for the coming together of the family. The holiday was always spent at the seaside. That was what children liked, Edgar assumed; and he himself took an almost instinctual – certainly unthinking – pleasure in gazing at the sea, watching wave after wave break and dissolve, hour after hour. He had to unwind, he said, to recover from the rush of business life. So he was content to sit on the beach, seldom even taking a dip (he was a poor swimmer). But the children liked to swim. They also liked, when they were small, to collect shells and seaweed; when they were bigger, they liked boat trips and amusement arcades; bigger still, they read guide-books and wanted to go to ruined castles and stalactite caves. Iris went with them, leaving Edgar to his unwinding. She was bored by the sea, unless it was excitingly rough.

Then the children asked for holidays abroad. Edgar wasn't keen; he went abroad quite enough on business, he said. But, as usual when Iris could say that something was for the children's benefit, he gave in. Iris, John and Sheila conspired to find places that were on the sea, yet within reach of interesting towns. By skilful use of day trips, they saw Avignon, Florence, Venice. Edgar, staying on the beach, admitted that the sunshine was more reliable in the Mediterranean. He didn't ask what they had seen; they were welcome to all this gadding about in the heat so far as he was concerned. One cathedral, or one old painting, was the same as another to him. But John was entranced; he had a keen appreciation of beauty. And Sheila, though she sometimes drooped in the galleries, enjoyed the shops and cafés, the thrill of discovery.

Iris was proud of her children: John was obviously clever, Sheila was remarkably pretty. 'So she ought to be – she's your daughter, Iris,' people said. It wasn't a mere compliment; women said it as well as men. Iris was intrigued to find that she could think of herself as an attractive woman. At her best past thirty, apparently, like some women in novels. Edgar, she supposed, was too used to her to notice. She was resigned to his failing to observe a new dress or a new hair-style. The kiss he gave her when he came home was a routine. Making love was a routine too, a reaffirmation of the fact that they were married. Iris no longer enjoyed it much. But that, she thought, was because she didn't get much pleasure out of anything that didn't involve John and Sheila.

'Don't you like being told that you're beautiful?' asked Alan King.

Iris laughed and said: 'Of course I do.' He was driving her home from a concert at Guildford; the outing had been organized by friends, at a cheap rate for twenty tickets, and she'd gone by bus because Edgar had the car. Alan taught music at John's school and was said to have a future as a composer.

She did like it – certainly from Alan, who was younger than she was, extremely good-looking, and presumably not hard up. He stopped the car and made love to her, verbal love of course, with considerable style and eloquence; nothing of the sort had ever come her way before. She listened until there was a risk that her vague smile might look like a commitment. Then she said: 'That's enough now, Alan – you know perfectly well there's nothing doing.' He sighed and drove her to her door.

Later she wondered why she hadn't been tempted to start an affair with Alan. It would have been enjoyable, the children were used to her being out in the evening, certainly Edgar need never have known. But it was out of the question, here in Dorking – not so much because people might have found out (few would have been very censorious) as because it didn't go with her idea of herself, of the way she lived. It wasn't, quite simply, something that she wanted out of life.

Before going to sleep, she wondered too whether Edgar had other women. Curiously, it was the first time that this had occurred to her. It was hard to imagine, mainly because when he came home he never looked as though he'd been enjoying himself. Obviously, however, it was quite possible. Iris was a little shocked at herself when she found that she didn't really care.

She wanted to keep Alan King as a friend. Friendship – or the lack of it – had always been important to her; and she thought that it was important to most people, often more important than romantic love or the pleasures of sex. You read novels in which women suffered because they were unhappily married, or abandoned by their lovers, but you didn't read about women who had no friends. And to go through an entire life without friends, it seemed to Iris, was a real desolation.

Luckily, she had plenty of friends. She was glad that she'd come to live in Dorking, after all. It was a friendly place – a place in which, since the excitements of a city were lacking, friendship was the nutriment of life. She made friends with neighbours (in London, she'd known nobody who lived in her block of flats); with the parents of children who went to school with John and Sheila; and with other people whom she'd got to know so naturally, in this environment, that she couldn't remember how she'd first met them. Most of her friends were married couples, and naturally she knew the women best, but she got on pleasantly with the men.

Almost every day, she had morning coffee or afternoon tea with a friend – at her house, at the friend's house, or at the Kardomah in the High Street. Every week, she was invited to dinner or to a party. When the children were small, it was easy to get baby-sitters; when they were older, they were often out themselves, for they too had plenty of friends. Edgar was invited too, but it was understood that he was seldom able to come. When he did come, he took little part in the conversation, which tended to run on local affairs.

'I'm sorry to unload this on you, Iris, I just had to talk to somebody.' Two women, quite recently, had said that: Moira Edwards, whose husband drank, and Jane Durbridge, whose daughter was pregnant. These acts of trust were good for Iris's self-confidence. She had friends – close friends. If ever she had troubles of her own (though she didn't foresee any) she wouldn't be alone. She recognized that she wouldn't dream of discussing Moira's or Jane's problems with Edgar. And if Sheila were pregnant, or if John got a girl pregnant, she would cope with the situation without telling Edgar. So her husband wasn't a close friend? She had never reflected on this; she didn't see the use of reflecting on it now.

The Council was going to close the primary school near the Blakes' house. Iris wasn't affected, since John and Sheila were at grammar school, but she thought it was wrong; young kids would have to cross a dangerous main road. A friend asked her to join a deputation to the Education Committee. She was surprised by the idea that her presence would be an asset, but she said she would go along. She was surprised, too, to be confronted by her wine merchant and a man with whom she'd played bridge – she hadn't realized that they were Councillors. She hadn't intended to say anything, but when another Councillor made an obviously absurd statement, she put him right politely and clearly. 'You were terrific, Iris,' her friends said afterwards. She laughed, but secretly she was quite pleased with herself. The school was reprieved. It wasn't the sort of thing that interested Edgar, so she didn't mention it to him.

John and Sheila both got into university, though it was a bit of a scrape for Sheila. Iris missed them, but time never hung heavy on her hands, and their absence made less difference than she had expected. More than anything else, she missed going on holidays with them; they naturally preferred to go off with friends. A holiday alone with Edgar – the first since their honeymoon – proved unfortunate. He got a stomach upset, blamed the French food, was outraged by the doctor's bill, and declared that he wasn't going abroad for his holiday again. Iris said that, since their tastes were different, it might be sensible for them to take separate holidays. He agreed quite readily. (Perhaps he did have a mistress? Not necessarily; he just didn't mind, more likely.)

From then on, he went to Bournemouth every summer. Iris went away in October, missing the heat and the crowds. She teamed up with Moira, who was divorced by this time. Moira was an adventurous traveller, and introduced her to Greece and Morocco. Frankly, it was a long time since Iris had looked forward to holidays so much.

John studied the history of art – Iris hadn't realized that it was a subject in its own right – took a First, and got a job at the Glasgow Art Gallery. It was a long way off; Iris seldom saw him. She thought of visiting him there, but she wasn't sure that this would be tactful. She wasn't able to talk to him as she had when he was a boy. Children grew up and made their own lives – one had to accept that.

Sheila was a different kind of student – a militant. She took up extreme left-wing views and was carried out by the police (though fortunately not arrested) in the course of a sit-in. After her second year, she didn't go back to the university. She settled in London, living with a young poet. They were the leading figures in what was called a street theatre group. Edgar grumbled about her not taking a degree – with all the opportunities she'd been given, why couldn't she buckle down to it like John? – but he was rather impressed by her being in a theatre company. Iris didn't try to explain to him what a street theatre group was.

After several invitations had gone unanswered, Iris went to see Sheila. She and her 'bloke', as she called him, were living as squatters in a condemned house in Stepney. It wasn't so bad as it sounded; there was water and electricity, the squatting was tolerated by the Council. But Iris's efforts to get on sociable terms with Chris – the poet – were rebuffed. He prowled round the room scratching his private parts, he talked to Sheila as though Iris weren't there, and he used the word 'fucking' in every sentence. Iris realized that he was trying to shock her and drive her away; probably he came from a respectable working-class family. She blamed herself. Why hadn't she thought before putting on a blue tweed suit and a hat? Coming from Dorking, she was the one who had to show that she wasn't a stereotype.

She went once more, wearing trousers this time, but to no avail. Sheila said that Chris was writing and took Iris to a pub (Iris hadn't been in a pub since her days as an architect's secretary). It was crowded and noisy – almost impossible to talk.

'Well, darling, come home whenever you feel like relaxing for a bit,' Iris said bravely. 'You know you're always welcome.'

Sheila lit a cigarette and said: 'Let's face it, we don't have anything in common now, do we?'

Iris told Moira about this, but not Edgar. She hadn't told Edgar that Sheila was living with a man, nor about the squatting. It was understood that Sheila was working too hard to come home. As time passed, Edgar ceased to ask about his daughter.

John came home to say goodbye; he had a new job in America. It was news to Iris that America had some of the world's best art galleries. After a year, he wrote to say that he was married. After another year, he and his wife spent a weekend at Dorking on their way to Italy.

Francine was a formidable young woman (not so young, in fact; she was older than John and had two children by a previous marriage). She was extremely tall, wore spectacles with green frames, and talked as though delivering a lecture. She was, in fact, a lecturer in cybernetics. Iris and Edgar, fatally, looked blank at this.

As well as being 'into' cybernetics, Francine was 'into' ecology, macrobiotic food and Zen. The more she talked, the less Iris understood. She tried to follow, but Edgar – uncharacteristically – argued; Francine's didactic manner, which he had never met in a woman before, got under his skin. He sputtered furiously when he was told that building new housing estates was wrong ('the crime of urban renewal'), that white kids should be sent to schools miles away to mix with black kids ('bussing'), that young people who did badly at school should have university places ('open enrolment'), and that industrial progress should be halted ('zero growth'). 'The girl's crazy,' he complained to Iris. This seemed to be borne out by Francine's frequent references to her analyst. Iris too couldn't accept Francine's opinions; but what Iris thought didn't matter, for Francine was also 'into' Women's Lib, and Iris became a nonentity after admitting that she hadn't worked since her marriage. The visit ended with kisses and promises, but Iris knew that it would not be repeated for a long time, if ever.

Altogether, this part of middle life was a bad period for Iris. She had lost her children, and she hadn't the consolation – like some women – of drawing closer to her husband. Edgar was more often away, and more uncommunicative on Sundays at home. Far from discussing anything, they scarcely even exchanged information; he didn't want to talk about his work, and if she spoke of what she'd been doing he offered no comments or questions. Also, as she entered the menopause, she was often unwell. Because of this, they no longer made love. On the whole, Iris was relieved; it had become embarrassing to pretend to a pleasure that neither she nor he felt any longer. Yet it was a narrowing of life, the surrender of a basic claim to significance in their marriage.

But in other ways, her life was broadening out. Friends kept asking her to do things, perhaps because they sensed a need, perhaps simply because she had plenty of free time. And the more she did, the more she regained her health and energy. She looked after the Oxfam shop one day a week; she typed letters, brushing up her old skill, for charity campaigns; she ran stalls at fêtes and bazaars. There was always a shortage of people to do such things, apparently – that is, efficient and reliable people, as Iris was, or so she was constantly assured. She answered briskly that anyone who wasn't a cretin could do the job. This she didn't altogether believe, for she had come to know her value. In any case, she soon got requests that certainly were not made to just anyone.

Arthur Buckley – she knew him through charity work, and he was active in the Conservative Association – asked if she would stand for the Council. Iris was astonished. She knew nothing about local government and she wasn't a political animal – she wasn't even sure if she was a Conservative, though she usually voted that way. Arthur said that he wanted candidates who were good citizens trusted by their neighbours, not political fanatics. Iris refused, however; she didn't like to wear a label nor to be placed in opposition to some of her friends (Moira voted Liberal). Then Arthur put another proposition: was she available as a co-opted member of a Council committee? When this was explained to her, Iris agreed. She was put on the Library Committee.

Over the next few years, other civic duties followed. She was entrusted with visiting and reporting on homes for children in Council care. She was co-opted on to the Education Committee; she gathered that her 'fight' (so it was now called) to save the local school was remembered. And she became a Governor of the girls' grammar school, where Sheila had gone.

She found that she enjoyed responsibility. It was satisfying to make a difference to the way things were done, and it was seldom hard to reach a sound judgement. She enjoyed committee meetings, too. There was an art in carrying a point without alienating people, and since she encountered other committee members who were pig-headed or muddled or illogical, it wasn't conceited to realize that she was above the average. At home, she turned a corner of the living-room into a sort of office, typed her reports neatly, annotated documents, and prepared carefully for meetings. The doorbell and the phone rang frequently; if she'd ever been in danger of loneliness, she certainly wasn't now. She made fresh acquaintances, some became friends, and a few of the friends became close friends. Quite often, people whom she didn't know – but who recognized her – stopped her in the street with a request. She laughed, but didn't dissent, when Moira said: 'You're a figure in the community.' For Dorking, when one got about it as much as she did, was a community. Hitherto she had seen only individual lives and family problems; now she saw them as interdependent, a harmony in need of continual adjustment and attention.

After being asked twice more, she decided that she would stand for the Council after all. But, by the time the election came round, Edgar had told her that they were to leave Dorking.

Edgar had never been against her community work. In principle, he lumped Councils with Government departments as a hostile force which he described as 'they'. 'They' made irritating rules and regulations, levied punitive rates and taxes, and were irrelevant to the real work of the world – the sort of work that he did. He conceded, however, that there had to be schools, public libraries and foster-homes, and someone had to see that they were properly run. It was a suitable task for those who were not otherwise occupied, for example women whose children were grown up. To put it simply, he didn't mind what Iris did to fill her time.

But she knew that he attached no real importance to it. He wasn't even aware of how much she did. When she told him that she'd taken on a new responsibility, he said: 'Oh, really? That's good' – and then, for all that she knew to the contrary, forgot about it. Some of her jobs, especially when they were temporary and linked to a specific occasion, she didn't mention to him. So it never crossed his mind that her activities should be taken into account when they made a change in their personal lives. He was retiring – that was the change. They were going to live in the real country, near the sea. They had lived in Dorking because it was within daily reach of London, and because the big house had been suitable for growing children. It would have seemed to him absurd to stay in Dorking just because Iris wanted to be a Councillor. He would have said, indeed, that it was selfish on her part. But they never quarrelled, so he didn't have to say this.

So here she was, walking along the straight unshaded road, from the village where she was a stranger to the house where she was equally a stranger. From nowhere to nowhere.

Despite such moments of depression, which came upon her without warning from time to time, Iris got through the next six weeks pretty well. The weather was sunny, and not always oppressively hot. Though she sometimes felt lonely in a house without neighbours, she got to know the regular traffic along the road: men going to work on tractors or bicycles, the bus, the post van, the shop on wheels. When she went into towns and villages, the pavements were even crowded. Most of the people were summer visitors, but this reassured her that she wasn't altogether cut off.

There was still a certain amount to be done in the house before she had it as she wanted it, and there was a great deal to be done in the garden, utterly neglected for two years. The soil had to be thoroughly dug over, nettles and docks rooted out, the brick path weeded. The garden (like the house) was smaller than the one she had lost, and space had to be left for a lawn, but she decided to plant as many flowers and shrubs as she could find room for. So far as possible, she would have something in flower at every time of the year, to brighten the outlook. She spent a happy afternoon at a nursery and came home with the back of the car crammed. Then she planted and planted until her arms ached. It gave her a sense of creation, of infusing life into deadness.

As Iris had renounced her usual holiday abroad, Moira came to stay for a week. It would be better to have her before Edgar settled in, Iris felt. 'You look run down,' Moira told her. 'You're going to have a good rest this week.' And in fact Moira did the housework and cooking. But soon the eager tourist in Moira came uppermost; the two friends spent most of the time driving round Norfolk, looking at churches and stately homes. Meanwhile, they talked and talked. Iris broke down in tears once and told Moira the worst – she hated leaving Dorking, she would never feel at home in Norfolk, she was condemned to useless idleness. Then she said: 'There, that's done me good. I'll be all right really, don't you worry.'

Edgar came every weekend and behaved as he always had during weekends at Dorking: he read the Sunday papers, he did the crossword, and he did some business work. Iris showed him the new carpets and curtains and the embryonic garden; he expressed approval without making any other suggestions. It was as though he were a visitor, being polite to his hostess. Didn't he know – didn't he feel, anyway – that he was going to live here? But then she thought that he was probably content to find the house waiting for him, as he had imagined it. In precisely this way, when they were married, he had let her furnish the house at Dorking as she chose. He didn't involve himself in making a home, in nurturing its growth.

She wondered if she was making a mistake by doing so much. It might have been better to wait for Edgar so that they could start from scratch, together. Digging the garden, for instance – that would have kept him busy for days. But what was she to do during these weeks, all alone here? The work was a necessity for her. And, whereas Edgar had wanted this home, she had to bring herself to accept it, by investing her thought and her labour in it.

Usually, on Sunday afternoons, they went to the coast. As Edgar had said, there was a magnificent beach – miles of sand, warm to the touch of bare feet under the sun. The approach road was thick with cars, it was difficult to park, and on the beach itself Edgar's rest was disturbed by children playing ball games. But he said: 'Ah well, we'll have it to ourselves when the holidays are over.'

So, almost before Iris expected it, they reached the last day of Edgar's working life – a Friday, of course. She went to his office in the afternoon. She had been there occasionally, perhaps a dozen times over the years, to meet him for lunch when she came up to town for a day of shopping or to see an exhibition; but she wasn't surprised when the receptionist failed to recognize her.

She found Edgar and went with him to the chairman's room, where drinks were handed round. About a dozen of the senior staff were there. As Iris was introduced and shook hands with them, she thought: how curious, these are men with whom Edgar has spent every day for years – some must be friends, even close friends – and I'm meeting them for the first time.

The chairman made a speech, along predictable lines. He presented Edgar with a set of ivory chessmen and Iris with a cameo brooch. Iris wondered whether the gifts came from some central stock, or whether Edgar had been mixed up with another man who played chess. Well, they could always sell the set. Also the brooch – it was fairly hideous.

They had another drink, shook hands again, and left.

Iris wanted to change before dinner, so they went to the hotel where Edgar had been living. As it was still August, the lobby was full of Americans, Germans, Japanese. It was odd, she thought, to be staying at a hotel in London, the city where she'd been born and brought up. After birthday dinners or theatres in the past, she had always gone home to Dorking.

They went to Prunier's. At first the head waiter said that he had no reservation for them; it turned out that the name had been taken down over the phone as Black instead of Blake. Edgar was very cross. Having ordered, he wrapped himself in a sullen silence.

'I liked your chairman,' Iris said.

'That's more than I do.'

'Well, they all seemed sorry to be saying goodbye to you, dear. I think they meant it, some of them anyway, when they said you must keep in touch. We could ask them down for weekends. We've got a spare room.'

'I don't know. Out of sight, out of mind, that's how things go.'

'They're your friends, after all,' Iris said desperately.

'Well . . . they're not bad chaps, I suppose.'

In the taxi going back to the hotel, she stroked his hand and said: 'I know how you must feel, darling.'

'I'm just tired,' he said. 'I didn't let up all day, you know . . . tidying things up.'

It was raining when they got to Norfolk next day. Just what you'd expect, Edgar said – Bank Holiday weekend.

The next two days were fine, but they didn't go to the sea because of the crowds. They read the papers; they walked along the road, in one direction on Sunday and the other direction on Monday; they watched television. On Tuesday they decided to go to the sea, but it rained again.

So their new life began. Was it a new life, however, or merely a cessation of the old life, with nothing to take its place? Iris couldn't guess how Edgar would have answered this question – if he had posed it to himself, which (so far as she knew) he didn't.

According to an article she had read, and noted particularly because it was soon after Edgar first spoke of his retirement, release from the demands of work caused a natural slowing-down. A man did everything at a more leisurely pace, without conscious intention. This didn't prove to be true of Edgar. He still shaved and dressed quickly. He still bolted his food as though he were late for an appointment. If he took on a job, such as weeding the path, he did it hastily and carelessly. When they went out in the car he drove fast, as he always had. One would have thought that he was being timed, or timing himself, over the two miles to the village.

On the other hand, he didn't seem to suffer from inactivity. He was capable – as he'd always been capable when on holiday – of sitting perfectly still for a couple of hours, body slackly relaxed, face expressionless. If Iris asked him what he was thinking about, he replied: 'Oh, nothing.' Any suggestion for doing anything, whether an outing or a project in the house or the garden, always came from her.

They went somewhere almost every day. So far as Iris was concerned, she simply wanted to get out of the house. At Dorking she had saved time by shopping in bulk and putting food in the deep-freeze; here she shopped as often as she could, to gain human contact. The village shops were so rudimentary that she often had a reason – or an excuse? – to go to the town. Edgar came shopping with her for the first time in his life. He was an impatient shopper, overtaking in the supermarket as though he were driving his car, drumming with his foot when he was kept waiting in the smaller shops, barking: 'That the lot?' to Iris. After a few weeks, he left the shopping to her. He sat in the car, or else stayed at home.

They went to the beach; it was a real pleasure on fine September days. They went to parts of the countryside that were supposed to be attractive – though it was all pretty dull compared to the North Downs, Iris thought – and they picnicked and did some not very ambitious walking. They went to the stately homes that Iris had seen with Moira; Edgar commented mainly on the probable cost of marble fireplaces and painted ceilings.

After one abortive expedition – they drove twenty miles to a stately home on a Tuesday, the only day when it was closed – he said that they would have to cut down on all this gadding about, with the cost of petrol what it was nowadays. Iris replied that they could drive slower, or indeed get a smaller car. 'Oh, we haven't come to that yet,' he said. He was very attached to the Rover. But if they were going out for the sake of going out, he didn't see the point of it.

The truth was, the house was enough for him. Iris had no right to be surprised. Just as he had never lived in Dorking in the same sense that she had, he wasn't interested in living in Norfolk, but merely in what he thought to be a suitably located house.

She found the evenings the hardest time to get through. She had always watched television selectively, and she was irritated by Edgar's habit of leaving the set on (like a child, she thought) whatever came up: comedy, costume drama, American detective serials, the early news, the main news, the late news. Sometimes, after inner hesitation, she made bold to ask: 'Are you keen on this, really?' He would say: 'Not really, I suppose,' and switch off. But then the sudden silence seemed cheerless, a space that she had no way of filling.

Since they had the chess set, she suggested that Edgar might like to take up the game. She had learned as a child – her father had been a keen player – and had played intermittently with various friends, as well as with John during his boyhood. Edgar picked up the rules easily, but he couldn't develop the ability to plan more than one move ahead, or else couldn't be bothered. He made his moves hastily, as if they had a limited time for the game, so he was liable to suicidal blunders. 'Have it back, dear,' Iris would say. But, though he was obviously angry with himself, he refused: 'No, no, I've done it now, haven't I? Got to stick to the rules.' So the game was soon over. Iris sometimes refrained from taking advantage of his mistakes, or even made deliberate mistakes herself, but that made the game so childish that it bored her. There was an irony about the whole idea, anyway. She had thought of it to give Edgar a new interest, but she was the one who needed diversion.

Her main solace was reading; indeed, when she was first faced with exile from Dorking, she'd found some comfort in the thought that she would be able to read all the books for which she'd never had time. While alone in the house, she had inspected the nearest public library and found that it was fairly good. It was twelve miles away, but an exchange of books could be timed to fit in with a shopping trip.

'I'm going to the library tomorrow,' she told Edgar soon after his arrival. 'You must get something for yourself.'

He acquiesced, as he acquiesced about the stately homes and the chess. But he had no idea what to choose.

'What did you read on those long plane journeys?' she asked.

'Thrillers, sometimes.'

She discovered that he had never read what she regarded as books that everybody had read. So she recommended *David Copperfield*. Interrupted by television and by his spells of reverie, it took him a long time to get through. Apparently – what a lot she hadn't known about him! – he was a slow reader. Perhaps that was why he'd spent so much time on his business papers. Iris herself was a fast reader. They used to sit facing each other in the two armchairs, he plodding along with *David Copperfield*, she racing through the latest Muriel Spark or Edna O'Brien.

'Did you enjoy it?' she asked when at last he'd finished.

'It's all right. A bit old-fashioned.'

What they didn't do was to talk: really talk, as Iris had talked with Moira and her other friends. From time to time, Edgar made remarks about the iniquities of the Government, or a crime that was in the news, or the cost of something they'd bought. Iris tried to build up a discussion, sometimes by disagreeing when she didn't really differ from him. But that wasn't his purpose; the remark had been a statement, complete in itself. If she broke the silence with a remark of her own, he usually agreed with her: 'Yes, that's right.' If she asked his opinion he gave it briefly, as though he were at an office conference.

They had never had much chance to talk during his working life. That had been a deprivation, surely, although she hadn't felt it acutely and he obviously hadn't. Now that they were constantly together, with all the time in the world, she felt that they ought to be talking in a way that justified the opportunity. About what? She wasn't sure. About their fundamental beliefs, about their real feelings . . . about life. But she didn't know how to begin, nor how to plant this conception in his mind. He had always used language as one might use the telephone, to convey what was immediate and essential. Evidently, he was content with that.

Well, Iris thought, perhaps it wasn't a good idea for two people to be alone together all the time. She had always been good at making friends, and if Edgar apparently didn't need friendships, he would acquiesce in them. Living in this remote house was a handicap, but Norfolk people didn't seem unfriendly. Already she had achieved conversations – superficial, of course, but amiable – with a few: the doctor with whom she'd signed up, the librarian, a couple of shop-keepers.

The way people talked about Norfolk, however, discouraged her. They all said it was quiet. Some – young people, such as the garage attendant where she bought petrol – said this in a discontented tone and were clearly longing to get away. Others said it smugly, even proudly, as a settled fact which newcomers must learn to accept.

She couldn't come across any of the kind of people she had known in Dorking: active middle-class and middle-aged people, immersed in local affairs. There were, so far as she could make out, three kinds of people in the 'real country'. There were landowners, deeply rooted in long tradition, who lived in houses called something Hall. They ran their farms, actively or through managers, and Iris supposed that they went in for hunting and shooting, but they also dominated the Council. Clearly, this was a world to which she couldn't gain entry. There were working people, not so much working on the land nowadays as in factories to which they made long daily journeys. Iris wasn't a snob, she hoped – she had got on well enough with trade union representatives on committees – but these working-class people made up another self-enclosed world, and she didn't see what she, still less Edgar, could find in common with them. Finally, there were retired people who had bought converted cottages like hers. When she saw them in the village, they all seemed to be much older than she was, older than Edgar too. They walked with difficulty (arthritis, she supposed) and spoke in quavering voices; she shuddered when she thought that she might reach this condition. In any case, they couldn't be expected to get about much.

So there it was. No one was likely to seek her help or enlist her in any activity. No one was likely to ask her to tea or a coffee morning or a party. She might have acquaintances, but not friends.

In October, the weather changed abruptly. It rained hard, sometimes from morning to night, sometimes for days together. Dark, heavy clouds rolled above the open landscape. Pools, fringed by mud, formed in the immense fields, on the road, and in the Blakes' garden. When it wasn't raining, a bitter north wind blew unchecked from the sea. The sky was either dark or a monotonous impenetrable white, and always sunless. Wet or dry, it was cold. Moira sent a postcard from Crete.

On one of the dry days, Edgar and Iris went to the beach. It was entirely deserted; there was a certain grandeur to the bare perspective and the long, thunderous waves. But they were frozen after a short walk, so they didn't go again. Indeed, Edgar said that there was no sense in going anywhere unless it was absolutely necessary. It wasn't necessary, in his view, to drive twelve miles to change library books and buy food. They could manage with what was in the village shop, or for that matter the shop on wheels.

Iris said that she didn't mind the drive; he could stay at home if he preferred. However, the car sometimes refused to start. It had always been garaged at Dorking, and it didn't like being left out in the rain. Edgar cleaned the plugs and fiddled with the carburettor – he was no great mechanic – but it was still unreliable. The garage owner would come out only after long delay and charged outrageously.

Without the car, one could take the bus to the village and return on the next bus five hours later, or one could walk through the rain. And there was nothing in the village, anyway.

It was even cold indoors. The living-room had open fireplaces, and Iris had always thought that a fire was one of the pleasures of the 'real country', so they bought a load of logs. Edgar sawed them with a resentful expression; living in the country, for him, hadn't meant adopting the simple life. The logs were damp and the fire never burned properly, so they went back to keeping the electric heater on all day. But the house still wasn't comfortably warm. It had draughts, they discovered, which hadn't been noticeable in summer.

'Couldn't we spend a few days in London while we've got this awful weather?' Iris asked.

'We can't afford to do that too often, you know,' Edgar said. 'We might go in the winter, when it's really cold.'

He cursed the weather as he cursed the Government and the cost of living: 'Bloody rain again – I'm fed up with it!' But he didn't really find it hard to endure. Having voiced his displeasure, he would say: 'Oh well, it's the swings and the roundabouts. We'll enjoy the summer all the more.'

But Iris found herself overcome, every few days, by hopeless, unnerving depression. She stood at the window, staring at the rain, feeling that she was doomed to stand there for ever, turned into a lifeless statue. Or she felt sobs rising in her throat, and ran up to the bedroom to cry without Edgar's knowing. She went to the doctor and got some tranquillizers, which made no difference. There was nothing wrong with her, after all, except her situation. She decided that she must draw on her reserves of fortitude. She had been through a bad time before, when she was plagued by the menopause and deprived of John and Sheila, and she had pulled herself together. True, she'd had friends and a busy life then, and now she had neither. But she must survive, she must live – she wasn't old. She had been here only a few months, not long enough to regain her balance after her world had changed. With time and courage, she would win through.

She read with fixed determination, but she couldn't read all the time, and there was one miserable wet day when she had finished her books and the car wouldn't start. She listened to talks and music on the radio, but turned it off after a while, afraid that it was becoming a drug. What she had to do, she decided, was to find ways of keeping herself active. She had bought her clothes for years, but now she set up her sewing-machine and made some new dresses. She studied recipes and, within the limitations of what she could buy, tried a bit of fancy cooking. Whenever the rain stopped, she worked in the garden.

Nevertheless, there were days when she could hardly force herself to dust the rooms and make simple meals. Days when her thoughts weighed her down, yet she couldn't think coherently. Days of emptiness, subtracted from her life.

Her enemies were loneliness and silence. The newspaper was dumped on the doorstep before they got up, there was often no post for them, of course there were no visitors; so they didn't hear another voice unless they went to the village. And the silence – it made her feel that the rest of the world had ceased to exist. Only, now and again when she least expected it, an aeroplane streaking over the house made a brief and deafening sound. There was a fighter station nearby, something else that they hadn't known when they bought the house. It was an alien and inhuman assault, mocking her defencelessness. After the instant of furious noise the silence returned, more still and vacant than before.

Edgar seemed to feel nothing of what she felt: neither depression nor loneliness nor even boredom. He read (*Vanity Fair* after *David Copperfield*). He listened to the radio, though he probably didn't try to follow the music. He did a few desultory jobs about the house, such as trying to track down the draughts, sellotape in hand. And he . . . did nothing.

'Aren't you bored?' she asked sometimes.

The question seemed to surprise him. 'Well, sort of. We might go for a walk if it clears up. Not long now till tea, anyway.'

She thought about him – secretly, as it were, and trying not to let him catch her looking at him. She was puzzled. Did he possess, at some hidden level, a strength that she lacked? Or was he free from needs that she had thought innately human? Was this life of isolation and inactivity just what suited him, what he had always desired?

Essentially, she knew nothing about him.

It came to her that this was logical, because they had only just started living together. And she felt the kind of baffled curiosity that she'd felt as a girl without intimacies or experience . . . Iris Perrier. She remembered thinking about Paul Sinclair after leaving his flat, and wondering: who was he, this man who had entered her body? what were his thoughts? what did he believe in or want or hope for? Then, not much later, she had put the same questions to herself about Edgar Blake. But soon, unable to answer them, she had ceased to pursue them.

One day in November, a wild gale blew across Norfolk. Just after six in the evening, the electricity failed. The house was in absolute darkness. Not for long, of course – Iris had always kept candles, even in Dorking. It was gloomy, all the same. It was a strain to read by candlelight, there was no radio or television, and worst of all there was no heating. They had supper early and went to bed.

There was still no electricity in the morning. It didn't come on until the afternoon. Edgar was angry. Incompetence . . . nobody cares . . . nationalized industries . . . overpaid workers. . . .

Iris sat in the dim room, quite calm, in her sweater and overcoat. When he subsided, she said: 'You know, I don't really like living here.'

But she knew, as she spoke, that it was not the whole of what she meant.

Edgar at once became reasonable. 'Well, after all, these things do happen. Could happen anywhere.'

'Yes,' she said. 'The truth is, we're not very successful at living together.'

He stared at her.

'What the hell d'you mean, Iris? We've been married for more than thirty years.'

She looked steadily at him.

'Have we?'

HAPPINESS IS . . .

As parents, the Talbots were concerned above all that their daughter should be happy. Carol grew up as a much-loved only child. An older brother had died in infancy, but Carol was never told about this lest it should worry her. She herself had a serious illness which involved many visits to doctors and clinics, and several periods in hospital, from the age of nine to twelve. The fear that they might lose her – though the doctors said that it couldn't happen – was a lurking horror for the Talbots, and they were immensely relieved when at last the disease was conquered. Partly because of the spells in hospital and partly because of a tendency to go off into day-dreams, Carol didn't do well at school although she was undoubtedly intelligent. Her parents didn't press her; the important thing was for her to be happy.

They lived in Wimbledon, in a detached house with a big garden. Mr Talbot was a chartered accountant. As a young man he had entered what he thought to be a safe, steady profession, but with the boom in tax avoidance he had become quite wealthy, without really meaning to. Their style of life was comfortable and not at all ostentatious. They felt most at ease on summer afternoons, having tea in the garden. Mr Talbot sat in an old-fashioned deck-chair, Mrs Talbot in an old basket-chair, and Carol on a rug on the lawn. Gazing at the sky through the leaves of the two tall beech-trees, one could hardly believe that one was in London.

When Carol was in her teens she did much better at school – no anxieties about O-levels and A-levels. She was a quiet girl, fond of reading, serious and thoughtful. Often she had an abstracted look on her face, but it was no longer a matter of day-dreaming.

'Deep thoughts, my dear?' her father would ask, stirring his tea.

'Well . . . I was wondering if it's ever justified to put a person in prison for life.'

Or: 'I was wondering, do people always need somebody to hate or will everybody get over it one day?'

Carol's parents were made rather uneasy by such questions and tried to divert her with a joke. They were tolerant, civilized conservatives; they knew that the world wasn't ideal and never would be. If you worried about everything that was wrong, you only made yourself unhappy.

'It would be nice if she had a boy-friend,' Mrs Talbot said.

'Oh, there's plenty of time for that,' Mr Talbot replied. Like most loving fathers, he didn't altogether like the idea.

'I think she needs a boy-friend. The right sort, of course.'

It was 1960, one read articles about how quickly girls grew up nowadays, and so it was a little surprising that Carol had no boy-friend. She was an attractive girl. Though quiet, she wasn't shy; she was often asked out, sometimes by a boy and sometimes with a group. When lured by her mother into a confidential chat, she said that there were several boys she liked – as friends – but she didn't particularly prefer one to another. She was choosy, Mrs Talbot concluded. On the whole, that was all to the good.

But at eighteen, Carol did have a boy-friend. His name was Tony Mitchell and he was clearly the right sort. He could go along with Carol's serious moods – the Talbots, discreetly leaving them alone when he came to the house, could hear the murmur of earnest conversation – but he also had a sense of fun. For instance, he was an excellent mimic. When he did Richard Dimbleby or Malcolm Muggeridge, everybody was in stitches. Carol laughed much more often after she became Tony's girl-friend. He took her out of herself, the Talbots said.

They had been at the same school (though not in the same class) since childhood. As sometimes happens, they hadn't taken much notice of each other until they were in the sixth form, but the long acquaintanceship created a sense of relaxed intimacy. The Talbots were also friendly with Tony's parents – Mr Mitchell was a stock-broker. The two families lived five minutes' walk apart. It was handy for dropping in for tea or whatever was the next meal or to watch television, quite informally. If you couldn't find Carol she was at Tony's house, and vice versa.

To make things all the better, when Tony and Carol got university places, both studied in London and didn't have to leave home. Carol took sociology at the London School of Economics. Tony went to Imperial College, taking physics and electronics. For all his fun, he had definite ideas about his future career.

Mr Talbot had his doubts about LSE. Carol's streak of innocent idealism, he was afraid, could be easily exploited by the left-wingers who swarmed there. Sure enough, she was soon going on the Alder-maston march and urging her mother not to buy South African oranges. When there was a demonstration or a protest meeting at the School, she was in it. The society they lived in was selfish and immoral, she said – surely Daddy could see that, when he met all those rich men trying to dodge paying taxes. She declared herself a socialist, though she wasn't (thank goodness) a Communist or a member of any actual political organization.

Still, there was no need to worry too much. She was obviously happy at LSE – wasn't that the main thing? – and getting the best out of it. She didn't let the political activity take precedence over her studies, for she read more than ever and did well in exams. And she saw through the illusions of the radicals, their belief that they had only to shout to shake the foundations of capitalism. Particularly when she was with Tony, she was quite ready to see the funny side of it. So the Talbots reassured themselves that it was all part of growing up. It was fair enough to be on the Left when you were young; some of Mr Talbot's friends had been on the side of the Reds in the Spanish Civil War (though he himself hadn't) and had developed into solid citizens.

Tony was very good for her – no doubt of that. Although he was clearly very much in love with her, he wasn't possessive and he didn't complain if she went off to a meeting when he had counted on taking her to the ice-rink. Patience was one of his best qualities – a patience rooted in mutual trust, for there was never any question of her ceasing to be his girl-friend. His own political ideas were mildly left of centre and he generally took Carol's side in a discussion, though he didn't hesitate to disagree with her more extreme opinions. But of course there was no time for campaigns and demonstrations at Imperial College; science students worked terribly hard, as Carol recognized. Tony was a reminder to Carol of what life was really about, from a practical point of view. By his final year, he had a pretty definite promise of a job in a large research laboratory. He would be able to work for his Ph.D, while also earning respectably. Whereas Carol, though she wanted to work, wasn't clear what she could do after graduating.

The parents – both the Talbots and the Mitchells – naturally hoped that there would be a wedding as soon as Tony got his degree and his job. He and Carol were young, but they knew each other thoroughly and they were both mature for their years. They had gone away together for holidays and it was to be assumed (times had changed) that they slept together. Some young men, and some girls nowadays, felt a desire to play the field before settling down, but evidently that wasn't true either of Tony or of Carol. So there was no reason to delay what was in the logical and desirable order of things.

The Talbots could see their daughter in a little house of her own, or perhaps a flat to begin with, preferably not far from home. She would continue to sign petitions and boycott South African goods, but her wilder ideas would mellow under Tony's influence and through the force of practical realities. She would lead a more active life than Mrs Talbot or Mrs Mitchell had as young married women, and probably she would have an interesting and satisfying job, perhaps as a social worker – until the arrival of the children, already half-real in the minds of potential grandmothers.

That was what they wanted for her, Carol knew. It was what Tony wanted. Often, she wanted it herself. Yet she was aware of other desires, so different that she couldn't explain them even to Tony. These desires were broad and imprecise, and couldn't be called practical, but sometimes they seemed to her to be the only reality.

She wanted to experience, and to match herself against, the full range of the world's possibilities. She saw the world as marked by the blackest evil, and she also saw in it visions of infinite goodness. No one whom she knew was aware of the power, the immensity, of either the evil or the goodness. So everything they did was puny, weakened by their limited grasp. They scratched at ugly wallpaper, when they were imprisoned by massive walls. They opened tiny windows, while the pure air of mountain-tops was far above their heads. That was life, they said. That was to be her life, if she contented herself with it.

The radical students saw something, but not much. Carol had become impatient with them, and sometimes amused by them, because of their lack of imagination, which showed itself as a lack of proportion. They denounced bourgeois democracy,but they were perfectly comfortable in it, privileged by the measure either of the surrounding world or of history. They lavished their sympathy freely, but they had no insight into real suffering, the interminable suffering of a starving peasant or a refugee or a political prisoner – it would have broken them in a week. They spoke of revolution, but they knew nothing of the dangers, nor of the inspiring challenge, of a real revolution; they didn't expect it nor seriously want it. That was why they could get equally excited about any campaign – for nuclear disarmament, against apartheid, against the Common Market, for higher grants, against a reactionary visiting speaker, for better food in the cafeteria – and equally enraptured by any small victory. It was all play-acting really, all part of growing up, as her father said. And when it was all over, when they were no longer studentsà A few would become full-time political activists, campaigning for ever, still equally vociferous about solidarity with the Venezuelan guerrillas or stopping urban motorways, except that by degrees it would become a routine. The rest would look for jobs and 'settle down'. The brightest would end up as conservative professors at LSE, like the radicals of the 1930's.

No, she had much more respect for Tony, who didn't claim to be a radical. But the focus of his scientific research was just as tiny: research that would add a tiny sliver to the knowledge, perhaps the efficiency, perhaps the comfort and convenience, of a corner of the world. It was astonishing to her that people whom she knew to be kindly and well-meaning – her father, and Tony's father, and Tony himself – should yet be so indifferent to what shaped and enclosed their lives: the great evil, the great goodness. She would live with Tony in the confines of his love for her and his admirable qualities, able to 'discuss everything' like a modern wife, but unable to speak of what really mattered. Until her vision faded, smothered by contentment.

But she was in love with Tony? Yes; when she murmured to him: 'I do love you', it was with complete sincerity and warming pleasure. Yet she couldn't devote herself to this love, nor find a purpose in it. Love – her love and his – was scaled down by the limitations within which it had to exist. It didn't touch the great realities, the possibilities of understanding and experience. So in the end it was small, puny, like everything else.

While Carol was taking her finals, she was invited to a party by her professor, who led a public life in journalism and television. At this party there was a man named Frantisek Leber. He came from Prague, he worked for the Czechoslovak State Radio, and he was in London to acquire some music programmes from the BBC. They talked until the party thinned out. Then, as they had nowhere else to continue, she went to his hotel room, where they talked until five in the morning.

Frantisek looked at the sunrise, touched her hand for the first time, and said: 'Your professor will think perhaps we have gone to bed.'

'Let's do that, now we know each other,' Carol said.

At ten o'clock he had to go to the BBC, and she had to take an exam. She felt perfectly clear-headed. She had decided to marry Frantisek Leber.

It was generally agreed that Tony behaved very well. He had one talk with Carol, walking up and down her garden, and then he didn't try to see her again. To his parents, to her parents, and to friends in the neighbourhood he said firmly that Carol had a right to do as she chose. But it was obvious that he was hard hit. He wouldn't look at another girl, either straight away on the rebound, or after Carol went to Prague.

The Talbots, however, argued and pleaded with their daughter. She was throwing away her happiness, they believed, and went on believing whatever she said. She must know she would be happy with Tony, after being his girl-friend for three years. And all of a sudden . . . 'I don't want to say anything against the man,' said Mr Talbot, 'but really, you scarcely know him.'

'I know I'll be happy with him,' Carol said.

'But how can you be happy?' cried Mrs Talbot. 'Out there in a strange country! You can't speak a word of the language. You won't have any friends. You don't even know what the food's like.'

While they were sincerely concerned for Carol's happiness, the Talbots also felt the blow to themselves. They had loved and guarded Carol all her life, and now they were to lose her. They knew she had to grow up, they knew she'd be leaving home if she married Tony; but that meant an easy adjustment with compensating pleasures, especially for Mrs Talbot . . . popping round, helping her to furnish, looking after the grandchildren. Whereas – Prague! The Talbots, as it happened, seldom took holidays abroad and 'foreign' was a word of some strength to them. Carol hadn't travelled much either. Western Europe they could have swallowed; you could exchange letters quickly, phone if necessary, make a quick trip. But Czechoslovakia was not in western Europe. Worst of all, it was behind the iron curtain.

Secret police . . . show trials . . . labour camps. Nothing like that would happen to Carol, of course, especially as Frantisek had an official job. Still, it was a nasty atmosphere. Letters might be censored, western newspapers were forbidden. She'd have to get used to watching what she said, if only to avoid getting other people into trouble.

Besides, she wouldn't be living in the way she was used to. Apparently a radio producer earned the same as a factory worker – that was Communism for you! When Mr Talbot asked about Frantisek's prospects, Carol replied: 'They don't think in those terms, Daddy.' Frantisek lived in a small flat and it wasn't easy to get permission to move to a bigger one; everything was by official permission, of course. He had no car. People who wanted cars were on a waiting-list for four years. Communism!

All this would be of minor importance, the Talbots said to each other several times, if only they could be sure that Carol would be happy with Frantisek. But could they? They knew so little about him – and so did she. It wasn't like Carol to act impulsively, or to be swept off her feet. They couldn't avoid an almost superstitious feeling that she was under a kind of spell.

'Are you in love with him, really and truly?' Mrs Talbot asked.

'Yes, really and truly,' Carol said, smiling calmly.

'But darling, this time a fortnight ago you were sure you were in love with Tony.'

'This is different.'

'You can't be more in love than you were with Tony.'

'Not more, I agree. But this is different.'

How so, different? Carol didn't explain further.

With the best will in the world, the Talbots couldn't take to their prospective son-in-law when Carol brought him home to dinner. To start with, one couldn't treat him as a young man. He was twenty-nine, but his receding hair made him look older. He wasn't good-looking – a bony face with a beak of a nose (as well as being foreign, he was Jewish) and glasses. He spoke good English, though with a strong accent, and was very polite; but jokes evoked nothing from him but a thin smile, and they didn't feel at ease with him from the first handshake to the last. His composure, above all, was disconcerting. When he glanced at Carol he seemed to assume . . . not exactly possession but complicity, as though they had a perfect understanding which others couldn't penetrate. Tony, in three years as her boy-friend, had never given that impression. Frantisek also assumed that there need to be no further discussion about his marrying Carol. Strictly speaking he was within his rights, as she was twenty-one, but it was rather strange. He behaved as though it were the most normal thing in the world to go to another country, snatch a girl, and whisk her behind the iron curtain. But then, Carol too behaved as though it were normal. Her composure was as complete as his; it was the most striking thing about her during the whole family crisis, which she declined to see as a crisis at all.

'Is Frantisek a Communist?' Mr Talbot asked Carol.

'He's in the Party. He couldn't work for the radio without being in the Party.'

Mr Talbot forebore to comment on this state of affairs, and said: 'I suppose you consider yourself a Communist now.'

'In Czechoslovakia it isn't a question of being a Communist or not. It's a question of whether you have genuine political ideals or whether being a Communist just means upholding a power structure.'

This was not quite clear to Mr Talbot, but he noted that Carol talked as though she were already Czechoslovak.

Frantisek left for Prague, having finished his work with the BBC. Soon afterwards, when she got her visa, Carol went too. Her parents saw her off, Mrs Talbot in tears and Mr Talbot with a last solemn kiss. They were not to go to the wedding, as Carol had said that it would be a brief formality.

So she began her new life as Karola Leberova (Carol, or Karel, was a man's name in Czech). Her home, the small flat, was at the top of five flights of dark, stone stairs in an old block. The windows gave on to the courtyard. There was nothing to stare at, no distraction, and that was all to the good. She spent the first weeks learning Czech with intense concentration. Without work, in a city where practically all wives worked, she was still a visitor. She got a job translating technical handbooks for imported machinery. In the hard mid-European winter, she and Frantisek left the flat long before dawn to queue for trams going in different directions.

Frantisek had no family. In the course of a walk on Wimbledon Common, he had told Carol about his childhood. When the Nazis began to enforce the anti-Jewish laws, the underground movement arranged for him to be taken to the home of a forestry worker in southern Bohemia. It was miles from anywhere, surrounded by gloomy, silent pine plantations. The forester and his wife, elderly and morose, didn't like children, or for that matter Jews, and had no feelings about the value of saving a human life; they simply got a grim pleasure out of defying and outwitting the Germans. When anyone came near the house, Frantisek was hidden under a pile of sacks in a dark toolshed, sometimes for a whole day. The rest of the time, he worked hard chopping wood. After the war – his parents had been gassed, of course – he was placed in a training-school run by the trade unions. He had to begin by learning to read, at the age of ten. At fifteen, he emerged as an engine-cleaner on the railways. Later, someone turned up his file and discovered that his father had been a Communist, and since he also did well in intelligence tests and had a good record in the official youth movement, he was sent to the university.

It seemed to Carol that this harsh youth, so unlike her own, showed her the reality of the twentieth century. As she listened, she moved her hand over Frantisek's lean, bony body. The pleasant spaces of Wimbledon Common, the comfortable houses, the people exercising their dogs, and the family cars bowling along the Kingston by-pass faded into an illusion with which she could well dispense.

In Prague, she grasped and clutched this hard, strong sense of reality. Politics was not a specialized interest nor a romantic enthusiasm, but a daily experience. This experience was so universal that people understood one another intuitively, with wry smiles and shrugs. There was no escape into private joy or private ambition. Life was regulated at every point by what her father called Communism – though it wasn't Communism but, as Frantisek said, 'bureaucratic deformations'. The human spirit, like a coiled spring, pressed stubbornly against the leaden weight of arbitrary power. People had no time for trivial chatter; they were often silent, and when the occasion was right they spoke seriously and from the heart. She and Frantisek had no circle of casual acquaintances. They had a few friends, to whom they were very close.

This new life wasn't – she hadn't expected it to be – better than life in England. By any comparison, it was worse. Yet, in an authentic and important way, it was lived at a higher level. It was a stride ahead. The social system had, after all, been transformed, even though the promise of that transformation had been terribly distorted. One didn't have to waste time on the catch-phrases of illusion: 'It's a free country . . . you make your own life . . . I'm not interested in politics . . . things aren't ideal, they never will be . . . worry too much, you'll only make yourself unhappy.' Here, to worry was to assert life and faith. Thought burned white-hot in the crucible of reality. The promise and the 'deformation' were locked in an eternal silent struggle.

Frantisek and Carol, with their friends, talked for hours at night in the little flat. Imagination, surging through their words, carried them into a future still to be won. They nurtured the dream, the vision of the world's goodness. It was an integral part, an essential condition of the way they lived in Prague.

They read and discussed books that sprang to life when released from the recesses of libraries: Proudhon, Rosa Luxembourg, Gramsci. In a box under the bed, they kept other books smuggled from abroad. Carol made translations in fat notebooks, working from midnight to dawn, writing in the bold, clear script of an English schoolgirl.

For her parents' sake, she went to London for a fortnight every August. She now had dual nationality; she had to get an exit visa, but could travel on her British passport. Frantisek didn't come with her, because permission wasn't given for a husband and wife to leave the country together.

'You look pale, dear,' her mother always said.

'I'm indoors all day, working.'

'Well, you must have a good rest. And eat properly, I'm sure you never do that out there. You're getting as thin as Frantisek.'

It was pleasant to lounge on a rug in the garden, gazing at the branches of the beech-trees swaying in the gentle English wind. Afternoon tea was pleasant, and Sunday lunch with a roast and baked potatoes, and playing rummy with her parents, and listening to the new records. Not real, but pleasant for two weeks in the year.

On her third visit, in 1967, she met Tony Mitchell as she was walking back from the swimming-pool. It was odd that she hadn't come across him before; probably he'd been away on holiday. He was embarrassed when she invited him in for a drink, but she soon put him at his ease.

Was he married? No. Did he have a girl-friend? Not really. It occurred to Carol that he was still in love with her, but she dismissed the idea as ridiculous. She was surprised that he wasn't married. True, he was only twenty-four. Carol too was twenty-four, but she had given up thinking of herself as young, in the sense of having life ahead of her – she was in the midst of it. She had changed, changed completely, though her parents pretended not to see it and Tony was too polite to say such a thing. And he was still what he had been: a nice boy.

Next year, imagination leaped upon the shoulders of reality. It was the Prague spring. Ideas, seeded in darkness, burst into the fresh sunlight. All that had been thought in secret, tacitly understood, became the open and general purpose. Nothing was secure, but anything was possible. Week by week, the gates of vision swung wider.

Books, pamphlets and newspapers were now the fertilizing agents of renewal. The radio and television were voices of hope. Frantisek and his friends were the trusted spokesmen of a people eager to be given words for its desires.

Carol dashed about, with Frantisek or on his errands, from the studio to the printing-press to enormous meetings. Her official job was now nominal; the boss was in eclipse along with other old bureaucrats and her colleagues were living as she lived, rejecting routine for adventure. Her political responsibility was helping the British and American journalists who swarmed into Prague – interpreting, guiding, explaining.

The best of them, she considered, was Bob Whitland. He was full of eager sympathy, but he understood the need not to exaggerate the new departures, not to provoke the watchful and suspicious power in Moscow. He took advice from Carol, joking that she was his censor. She used to hurry round to his hotel before he made his late phone call. 'This Bob is a little in love with you, I think,' Frantisek said. 'He's in love with all of us,' Carol answered.

Then her parents wrote, asking when they were to expect her for her annual visit.

It seemed absurd to miss a day of the Prague spring, now a blazing summer. But Frantisek said that she must go. She really needed a break. Somehow – it was one of the unforeseen chances of that time – she was pregnant. She was annoyed about it; the last thing she had time for was a baby. But there it was, and to make matters worse she had bad bouts of morning sickness. So she kissed Frantisek, kissed Bob, and went to London.

One morning, because of running to the bathroom to be sick, she missed the radio news. When she came downstairs, her mother held up the paper and said: 'This is bad, isn't it?'

The Russians had occupied Czechoslovakia.

Carol went to the office of Bob's paper and was allowed to sit with the copy-takers when he phoned his story. Then he talked to her. 'These kids are fantastic,' he said, meaning the young Czechs who were blocking the streets of Prague, clambering over Soviet tanks, explaining their truth to the soldiers. 'But I'm afraid it's hopeless. The Politbureau doesn't change its mind.'

Of course, the Russians had taken over the State Radio building. But the radio was still on the air, using hidden mobile transmitters. Carol listened to it whenever she could pick it up. Once she thought she heard Frantisek's voice, but the reception was bad and she wasn't sure. A week after the invasion, Bob told her that he'd received a message from Frantisek. He was all right; he sent Carol his love and said that she must stay in England. He was in the forests of southern Bohemia, where he had hidden as a child.

But resistance was hopeless, as Bob said. A new government was installed, order in the streets was restored, the radio was silenced.

Then Bob sent the news that Frantisek was under arrest.

It was impossible to find out where he was being held or when he would be tried. Bob did his best, but his sources were drying up. The editor dramatized the case, with big photos of Carol – 'The British Wife Who Waits'. She was dubious about this, but let herself be persuaded that it might help. The only result was that Bob was expelled from Czechoslovakia.

He came to see Carol as soon as he reached London. It was strange to sit with him in the peace of the garden at Wimbledon, after all their hurried, urgent meetings.

'Where are you going now?' she asked.

'I'll have a short holiday. I ought to see my parents, down in Dorset.'

'And then?'

'Nigeria, it seems. This Biafra thing.'

Indeed, Czechoslovakia was no longer the big story. Of the correspondents Carol had known in Prague, most had been recalled.

She didn't expect to get news of Frantisek for a long time. But apparently the men in power, or the Russian generals, wanted to strike swift blows and achieve an effect of intimidation. It was announced that Frantisek and three of his friends had been tried by a military court, found guilty of inciting armed rebellion with the aid of western intelligence services, and sentenced to death.

This brought Czechoslovakia, or at least Frantisek and Carol, back to the front page of Bob's paper. And obviously, now, there was nothing to be lost by a public campaign. Carol dashed about London as she had dashed about Prague. She was photographed at the door of the Czechoslovak Embassy, where nobody would see her. She got hold of prominent people – MPs, her old professor, television personalities, writers – to join in demands to free Frantisek Leber. In the midst of this activity, she had a miscarriage. It started in a taxi taking her from the BBC to the House of Commons; she had to tell the driver to make for the nearest hospital.

She didn't mind losing the baby, for she was clear-mindedly facing the inevitability of living without Frantisek. Even if he was reprieved, he would be in prison until there was a change in the political situation – a remote prospect. In fact, Frantisek was shot while she was in hospital. Bob's paper reacted to the news with clamant horror, mingled perhaps with professional appreciation of the dramatic coincidence.

After she had answered the letters of condolence and been suitably photographed at the memorial meeting, there was nothing for Carol to do but to sit in the garden, watching the leaves fall from the beech-trees. Her parents wrapped her in love, sympathy and tact. The tact consisted in avoiding all mention of Czechoslovakia. Carol was to grieve – that was natural – but not to worry about what unfortunately couldn't be helped. And she found herself yielding to this gentle pressure. Though she tried to keep up with whatever news still came from Prague, and to read serious books as usual, she turned with relief to nineteenth-century novels or listening to music. She was not at all well, what between general exhaustion and the miscarriage. Not at all strong, anyway. The doctor gave her pills and warned her that she needed plenty of rest.

Mr and Mrs Talbot confided to their friends, such as the Mitchells, that they were thankful to have Carol home again, though the reasons for her being home again were of course tragic. As always, they sought her happiness. It had been regrettably interrupted; but now, by degrees and with the aid of loving care, it could be restored. Carol understood perfectly well what they wanted for her.

But she couldn't be happy, she knew, by relapsing into the life that had failed to satisfy her before she met Frantisek. What they saw as an interruption had been her only experience of being fully alive. These idle weeks, lengthening into months, gave her the feeling – more than ever – that nothing around her was real. She snapped at her mother over small matters (this, naturally, was taken as further proof that she wasn't her old self yet). Afternoon tea, the nourishing meals she was made to eat, evenings watching stupid television programmes – all these made her impatient. She was even impatient with the English weather, as autumn slumped into a mild, damp winter. She missed the hard frosts.

Tony Mitchell was often at the house, dropping in as he used to when they were students. He would be taking his Ph.D in the coming year. After that he would have a good new job, or the prospect of an even better job if he chose to go to America; he hadn't decided about that. What did Carol think about America? Great opportunities, especially in science, Tony said; on the other hand there was the constant pressure, the rat-race. Carol didn't feel obliged to give an opinion.

Sometimes, when Tony came in the evening, Mr Talbot retired to his study to finish off a client's accounts and Mrs Talbot took a long time over the washing-up, just as they used to when Tony was Carol's boy-friend. He sat beside her on the couch; their bodies touched accidentally when one of them happened to move. He didn't try to kiss her, except on the cheek when he said good-night. He was part of the surrounding atmosphere of sympathy and tact – of love, she supposed – and of unreality. She understood that a return to her old life would mean, logically, a return to Tony.

'You're wasting your time if you imagine I'm taking up with Tony again,' she told her mother sharply.

Mrs Talbot was embarrassed. She was hoping that Carol would marry Tony, to be sure. But Frantisek had been dead for only a few months and it was too early to bring this hope into the open, as Tony doubtless appreciated.

'It's nice and cheerful with Tony here,' she said. 'You've been very unhappy, darling.'

'I'm not the same as I was before I married Frantisek, Mummy.'

'Well, dear, nobody's saying you should forget Frantisek. But you're still young. All we want is your happiness.'

In January Carol read a long article by a journalist whom she'd known in Prague in the summer, and who had just been back. He described the repression as merciless. But, he wrote, the Czechs showed no sign of being reconciled to their rulers. Illegal papers still circulated. The militants of the period of freedom were not all under arrest. Some were in hiding; others, dismissed from their posts and working in factories, were contriving to keep up the spirit of resistance.

Carol rang up the journalist and met him for a drink. She questioned him closely about the people he'd been able to trace.

He suddenly gave her a keen look and asked: 'You're not thinking of going back, are you, Carol?'

'Yes.'

'You're crazy. You'd be arrested at the airport.'

'Perhaps.'

She was asked to call at the Foreign Office. It was explained to her that, despite her dual nationality, the British Embassy could not undertake to protect her in present conditions.

She told her parents that she would like a holiday. Her health was practically normal by now; what she needed was a few weeks in the sun. An excellent idea, they said. Her mother offered to come, but Carol said that she would be quite all right alone. She hadn't decided where to go – the Costa del Sol, possibly Morocco. Her father wrote out a cheque, and she bought a ticket for Prague.

As she had no visa in her British passport, she showed her Czechoslovak passport on arrival. The official examined it carefully, but handed it back in silence. She took the bus to the city centre and then the tram to her home. It was snowing, and very cold.

She half expected to find the flat reallocated, but when she unlocked the door it was empty. Her other fear had been of seeing it exactly as Frantisek had left it. But Frantisek had been a tidy person, and the flat was in a mess, with books and papers all over the floor. Evidently it had been thoroughly searched.

Carol dumped her suitcase, lit the stove, and went out again to buy some food. She spent the evening putting the flat in order, dusting and cleaning. Then she went to bed, tired but contented.

The police came at five in the morning. Carol wasn't much surprised; it would have been silly for them to attract attention, including the attention of foreigners, by arresting her at the airport. They watched her while she dressed, made her stand on the landing while they searched the flat again, and then took her away.

The prison was old, like most buildings in Prague. The cell to which she was taken, after being searched to the skin, had stone walls, a tiny barred window, and a heavy door with a noisy lock. A real prison, she thought.

Standing on tiptoe to peer out of the window, she could see a rooftop loaded with fresh, brilliantly white snow. It was no longer snowing, however. The sky was a clear and beautiful blue.

In the early afternoon, so far as she could judge – her watch had been taken away – two guards came for her.

'Leberova – interrogation.'

Walking through the corridors, she felt perfectly calm, strong, and more genuinely alive than she had for months.

She was made to sit on a small wooden stool. The interrogator was smoking a cigarette and reading a document. When he was ready, he said: 'Leberova, Karola?'

'Yes.'

'We want to know about your instructions from the British intelligence service.'

Three hours later, when Carol was taken back to her cell, she found that she was stiff from her fixed position on the stool. Also, she couldn't see her way in the corridor properly after all that time staring into a powerful light. She didn't walk fast enough to satisfy the guards. One of them gave her a shove; she fell on the stone floor and bruised her face.

In the cell, she lay on the bed for a while, but she knew that this wasn't the way to get over her stiffness. She got up and did some exercises. She was hungry, having eaten nothing all day. But she could hear the other cells being unlocked; they were bringing the prison supper.

She rested her bruised cheek against the stone wall. She felt truly happy.